A RUDE AWAKENING

Wild Bill had enjoyed pleasurable dreams all night, drifting from the arms of Liddy McGinnis to the lips of Elena Vargas. Abruptly, a shattering crash sent fragments of the west window exploding into the room.

Before he was even fully awake, Wild Bill rolled off the opposite side of the bed, taken over by the survival reflexes of a cat.

Even as he hurtled toward the floor, Bill tugged his gunbelt off the bedpost. By the time he hit the floor, fully awake now, he had drawn a Colt and cocked the hammer. Still not sure what was happening, he used the bed for cover while he tried to confirm a target.

Wild Bill heard the hollow drumbeat of hooves in the street as a rider escaped. He saw the broken window and tensed . . .

WILD BILL

JUDD COLE

SANTA FE DEATH TRAP

LEISURE BOOKS NEW YORK CITY

To "General" Mike Mumford.

A LEISURE BOOK®

April 2000

Published by

Dorchester Publishing Co., Inc.
276 Fifth Avenue
New York, NY 10001

ISBN 0-8439-4720-9

SANTA FE DEATH TRAP

Chapter One

In the summer of 1874, J. B. Hickok found himself at loose ends—the victim of his own growing fame.

His hectic tour with Colonel Cody's show was a year behind him. That popular and publicized trip had ensured "Wild Bill's" status as a national icon. By now, however, his face was too famous, and his hide too valuable, to permit a return to his more anonymous life as a lawman.

But "fame" didn't automatically pay a man's poker debts. So after leaving Cody's show, Hickok sold his services to the highest bidder—Allan Pinkerton and his brand-spanking-new detective agency. Wild Bill became one of the nation's first "Pinkerton men."

For nearly a year Wild Bill survived Sioux warriors, cattle wars, railroad wars, escaped convicts, Mexican cutthroats, professional snipers and gun-throwers, and a hard-cussing hellcat named Calamity Jane. Then Hickok finally got his belly full of it and sent a curt telegram to Pinkerton. Bill informed his employer he was taking "French leave" until such time as he either returned to Denver or got himself killed, "whichever transpires first."

Hickok had his heart set on enjoying himself once again at one of his favorite frontier watering holes, the La Fonda Hotel in Santa Fe, New Mexico Territory. Bill took great pains, however, to keep this plan close to his vest. Even his sole companion on the trail, a young *New York Herald* reporter named Joshua Robinson, knew only that they were "headed south for a little sport."

"I just don't get it, Bill," Josh protested as the two riders spurred their mounts up out of a long cutbank that skirted Raton Pass. "Usually you like it just fine when your exploits get written up back east. You told me so yourself. Said it helps your love life. So how's come you muzzle me now?"

"Used to be it helped my love life," Bill corrected him. "Women are natural-born show-offs, so they love to intrigue with us 'living legends.' It gets their dresses and new bonnets described by you newspaper wags. But comes a point where all that three-penny fame just gets lead tossed at a man. Right now, kid, I just want a chance to *enjoy* that love life you ink-slingers have so vividly described."

"Well . . . don't you at least want folks back in the States to know where we're headed?"

"Actually, I'd sooner lose two jaw teeth, Longfellow. Now, pipe down, wouldja? I can't hear a damn thing above all your jabber."

Once their remuda string, four mustangs necked in pairs on a long lead line, cleared the cutback behind them, Bill reined in to make a good study of the surroundings. Hickok sat astride his favorite mount from their new string, a chestnut gelding with a roached mane and two white front socks.

Wild Bill's weathered eyes narrowed to slits in the glaring heat and sun of the arid Southwest. The trained vision of a veteran scout and stage driver took all of it in at once, not searching for anything specific, exactly, but just letting the entire vista "sneak up on me," as Bill had once explained the elusive art of scouting to Josh.

Way off on their right, pink-and-bluff cliffs dropped into redrock canyons so deep the floors were cut off from all sunlight by early afternoon. In the middle distance, the nearly barren hills had been gouged deep by jagged washes. Well to their left, a big, natural rock cistern was crowded with cottonwoods, cedars, and a riot of tangled blackberry brambles.

"Must be Santa Fe you've got in mind," Josh guessed for at least the dozenth time since they'd been on the trail. "That's where we're headed, isn't it? El Paso is too far for a pleasure trip, and Albuquerque is too flea-bitten. You're a man who likes clean sheets, so it must be Santa Fe."

Bill shook his head at the kid's irrepressible nosiness. Josh had just turned twenty and was still a clabber-lipped greenhorn. But Bill had to admit the youth was an immensely talented wordsmith. Unlike the far wealthier Ned Buntline, who cynically lied about his dime-novel heroes, Josh created breathless drama from real exploits. The kid was also a tolerable cook. That was another reason why a bunch-quitter like Hickok put up with his company.

"Kid," he finally responded, "you'll know where we're going when we finally get there. Ain't that soon enough? Now stow the chin wag and strip your rig. It's time to switch off."

"Aw, man alive," Josh carped. "Again? Cripes, I'm getting blisters from doing and undoing latigos."

"Blisters?" Bill repeated. "All this time riding with me, and you still got female hands?"

"You primp more than I do," Josh shot back, blushing at Bill's insult.

"So? I don't whine about blisters, do I, sis?"

Hickok was already down, dropping his bridle and headstall, while Josh still sat his horse, frowning and complaining. Bill's lips spread in a grin under his usually neat mustache, now somewhat dusty and shaggy from the trail. Much of his likewise dusty face was in shadow under the low brim of a black plainsman's hat.

"Hell, I know why you're bellyaching so much, Longfellow. Old Smoke's got it in for you. You're 'fraid to ride that broomtail devil, ain't'cha?"

The kid bit back his reply as he, too, dismounted and began stripping his rig from the docile, fifteen-hand piebald he'd ridden for the past two hours. In this heat, and with all the climbing they'd done in the past few days, Bill insisted on spelling the horses often.

Both men tossed their saddles and pads aside, then stretched the sweat-saturated saddle blankets out to dry in a wiry patch of grass. A gut bag tied to Bill's saddle horn bulged with water. They quickly rubbed the sweat off the tired animals, then watered all six horses from their hats—just a few swallows as a promise of more to come.

Bill studied the area carefully, then decided it

was safe enough to sprawl in the buffalo grass and smoke his last cigar while the blankets dried.

"It's got to be Santa Fe," Josh reasoned out loud as he plopped down beside Hickok. "Anyhow, I wish you'd just tell me. I can't file a story until I know."

"Yeah, I counted on that," Bill replied, his teeth clamped around his cheroot.

The kid winced as he spread petroleum jelly on his raw and ravaged hands. Much of this damage was simply from gripping reins. Bill had purchased these animals from a half-breed trader, impressed by their strength and stamina. But the backs of these damned, half-wild, Southwest mustangs could turn into hurricane decks in an eyeblink.

"My editor will read me the riot act," Josh complained. "He hasn't heard from me in—"

"Set it to music," Bill dismissed him, idly watching a ragged tatter of cloud drift across a seamless blue sky. But even while relaxing, Hickok rolled up onto one elbow every few minutes to scout the terrain.

"You expect trouble?" Josh demanded eagerly.

"What, eventually? Does a rag doll have a patched ass? But this time I'm hoping to stay just a few days ahead of trouble. See, I've got this appointment."

"With whom?" Josh demanded.

"Venus, if I'm lucky."

Bill sat up, stretched, then ground the cigar out carefully on his boot heel. He tucked the stubby remnant into his vest pocket.

Bill checked the blankets. They had dried quickly in this hot, dry, thirsty air that could extract liquid from jerky.

"C'mon, kid, quit malingering. We got to git. We can make it to a little pueblo called Chimayo before nightfall."

Josh's eyes sparked at this additional clue to their destination. He quickly extracted a dog-eared U.S. Army map from one of his saddle pockets. Josh had bought it up in Pueblo, Colorado, off an old man operating a wagon way-station. Made by a military cartographer, it showed key points throughout the vast Army Departments of Arizona and New Mexico.

"Chimayo," Josh repeated. "Chimayo . . . here it is. Yep! Just a little fly speck on the trail north of Santa Fe. Less than fifty miles north, I'd say."

"Actually, it's slightly northwest," Bill corrected him, requiring no map. Hickok knew the New Mexico Territory well from his youthful days as a stage driver operating over the old Santa Fe Trail. "Kid, damn it. I said it's time to raise dust. Stow that map and saddle your remount. I got to tie your damn boots for you, too? I want a shirttail brat, I'll get married and have one."

Josh scowled, but not at Bill's roweling. Now the real trouble would start again—the kind that had left Josh's tailbone aching for two days now. He had only two remounts besides his regular saddle horse, a well-trained sorrel. And now it was Old Smoke's turn to torment Joshua. The sturdy four-year-old gray was smart, but bull-headed, and wouldn't let a rider do anything without a fight. Old Smoke especially hated the belly cinch and knew plenty of tricks to thwart it.

Wild Bill tied his chestnut's bit ring to the lead line and selected a remount, a solid white mare. Normally Hickok avoided white horses because they were security risks after dark. But this one had been broken to halter by Tewa Indians. It had exceptional bottom on the long ascents because its nostrils had been slit wider for extra air. By now her lungs were greatly expanded, and Bill suspected she could gallop full-bore for ten miles or better.

The white easily took the bit, even lowering its head to help Bill with the headstall. He tossed on the blanket, pad, and saddle, meantime watching Josh trying to sugar-talk Old Smoke.

"Be sweet," the kid urged the gray, tossing the blanket across its sturdy withers. "Be sweet, and you'll get the currycomb and oat bag tonight, Smoke, wha'd'ya say, boy, huh?"

Bill bit his lower lip to keep from laughing outright. The fandango was coming. Bill continued to check his latigos, watching the kid from caged eyes.

"Atta boy," Josh soothed. His tone was gloating, for Old Smoke had taken the bit like an old cab horse. And now he stood patiently, flicking his bushy tail at pesky deerflies while the kid centered the saddle.

"Why, look, Bill. I've finally taught him who the master is," Josh boasted. "See that? Old Smoke didn't even sidestep when I cinched the girth."

"Yeah, he knows you're the boss," Bill said, grabbing leather and swinging up and over. "No doubt about it, kid. You're quite the *caballero*."

"Well, Bill! How do you like the Philadelphia Kid now?" Josh demanded after he'd mounted and reined the subdued gray about.

The youth, pumped up full of himself, let out a high-pitched yipping sound like a cowboy trying to turn a stampeding herd.

"Wild Bill Hickok said I had a round ass! Said

I'd never stay on this monster for two hours. Hear that, Smoke? Now I got you lipping sugar from my hand, and famous Wild Bill will swallow back his words for once. Let's head for Chimayo, boy. Gee up!"

Hickok, still grinning in wicked expectation, tightened his knees on the white's shoulders. Just a touch, and the trail-savvy mount was in motion. Josh was still out ahead, waving his hat and yipping to taunt Wild Bill.

But the kid hadn't noticed yet how Old Smoke was slyly angling off to the right—toward a spiny patch of prickly-pear cactus near the trail. He'd also failed to notice how Old Smoke sucked in a big breath just before Josh cinched the girth. That saddle, Bill realized, was on looser than a wet bow string.

Even as he grinned, however, Hickok felt a cool feather tickle the bumps of his spine. He'd felt such warnings before. Dick Wooten, the old Taos trapper, once told Bill they were "God fears," sent to a man as a favor by the Almighty. Wherever they came from, by now Bill knew better than to ignore them.

Cold, gunmetal-blue eyes like glittering chips of ice scoured the terrain. All seemed peaceful. But Hickok took a moment to slide each of his pearl-gripped Colt .44s from their holsters and check the loads.

" 'Bout this time tomorrow," Frank Tutt announced soon after draining his second bottle of sour mash, "maybe there'll be one less back-shooting Yankee coward in this world."

Despite Frank's boast, however, the young tough was a pitiful sight at the moment. He lay curled on his side in bed, clutching at his cramping stomach and trying not to retch. He'd ridden into Santa Fe early that afternoon, after several hard days on the trail. Elated by his recent discovery, Frank made the mistake of hitting the bottle before he ate anything.

To celebrate, Frank took a room at the Dorsey on College Street—Santa Fe's only other "better-class" hotel. Men of his ilk were not welcome at the Dorsey. But then, nobody on their staff had the guts to tell him that. So there was no problem, Frank figured. The only thing he feared was violent authority; nothing else even got his attention. To Frank, either you were a threat or you were just another one of the milk-livered "citizens" who paid taxes.

"Yankee?" scoffed Lisa Tipton. The pretty, over-painted sporting girl sat on the edge of the big bed. She wore only a lace chemise. Lisa scowled, and cursed under her breath, as she struggled to brush out her wildly tangled red hair.

"The war's long over, Frank," she added. " 'Cept in bed with you. Just look what you done to my hair, you animal! You're too rough, Frank."

Tutt ignored her, trying to understand how he could feel so downright awful in such a fancy room. True, the very finest lodgings in the West were available at the nearby La Fonda Hotel, of course. But Frank knew a strutting peacock like J. B. Hickok would stay at La Fonda. And Frank had a strict rule: Never kill where you sleep.

"I don't want you slapping me anymore, either," she flung at him. "We ain't married, you got no right to hit me."

"Pitch it to hell! You got paid, didn't you? Frank Tutt settles his accounts, by God. And whether it's tomorrow or not, I aim to settle one account damn quick."

The room's Oriental rug and newfangled flush commode notwithstanding, Tutt hadn't even bothered yet to change, bathe, or shave. Several days' worth of bristly beard smudged his face. He was a handsome man, but mean-looking around the mouth.

"Christ, I might hafta puke," Tutt groaned.

"Well, is it any wonder you're sick, you damned fool? Cold watermelon and hot whiskey don't mix so good in an empty stomach."

Lisa began to wiggle her supple hips into a corset.

"Who you mean to kill?" she asked him. "You wasn't in the war. You're just barely in your twenties now. The war's been over for almost ten years now."

"I was too young," Frank agreed. His voice was quieter now in a dangerous way. "But my big brother Dave wasn't."

"Frankie, darlin', don't be carrying no war grudge this long. Why, I lost two brothers at Antietam Creek, one fighting on each side."

Frank silenced her with a violent shake of his head.

"You don't know about it, woman, so whack the cork. I'm talking about murder in cold blood, not war killing. You want to know who it is I mean to kill? Well, just read the *New Mexican* in the next few days. They'll write it up big, I'll guaran-god-damn-tee they will. Matter fact? It'll even make big headlines in Paris and London when *this* jasper goes under."

"Sure it will, Frankie," the soiled dove humored her john. She met a lot of big talkers in her line of work. Although he was an obnoxious boaster, she knew Frank Tutt too well to push an argument too far with him. He was smart and tough and one of the most accomplished shootists in a land renowned for its marksmen. That's why he earned an impressive $100 a month working for the big *jefe* hereabouts, El Lobo Flaco, the Skinny Wolf.

But Frank also had a quick, nervous manner and a hair-trigger temper. Worse, he was a brooder with crazy, inconstant eyes. Rumor had it he cut a whore to death out in Tombstone after she called his organ "a little itty-bitty thingie." So Lisa always handled him like nitro.

"Frankie," she flirted, batting her eyelids and making a little moue. "Draw up my laces, please?"

The stays of her corset could only be tightened from behind. Lisa braced herself against one of the carved bedposts, her taut little derriere thrusting up provocatively. Frank groaned at the trouble. But he rolled out of bed, wearing only his dirty linen drawers. He squared off behind her.

"Good enough?" he gasped, giving the laces a strong tug that jerked her straight like a prisoner on the rack.

"Tighter," she choked out. "I can feel it'll go even tighter. Don't stop till my cheeks glow like apples."

"Crazy goddamn women," Tutt muttered, giving her stays another hard tug. He tied them with a strong double-hitch knot.

Frank tipped Lisa a silver dollar and sent her on her way. He decided to get dressed and shove some solid food in his aching gut. Frank still had a few things to take care of before Hickok arrived. Best of all, Frank didn't have to worry about hur-

17

rying it up. El Lobo didn't even know, yet, that Hickok was headed this way. Frank could drag it out awhile, like a cat pawing a doomed mouse. After years of waiting for it, revenge tasted much sweeter when it could be savored rather than gulped.

He had no doubt, by now, that Hickok would be coming within a day or so. Frank had been watching, hiding in his assigned observation post in the rimrock, when Hickok and the tenderfoot with him took the Cimarron Cutoff to avoid the rock-strewn Raton Pass. That meant they could only be headed toward Santa Fe—there was nothing else out here in the barren land of Coronado. At least, nothing a prissy like Hickok would care about.

No, it was clear enough. Hickok had chosen the City of Holy Faith to raise a little unholy hell. His conquests in Santa Fe were national legends: opera stars, singers, and actresses; a Spanish countess; a Norwegian princess; even haughty young heiress Katherine Vanderbilt, cousin to Cornelius himself. Now the stag was in rut again, Frank figured. And what city had been luckier for Wild Bill than Santa Fe?

Tutt's face went granite-edged with hatred. His eyes cut to the Colt Navy revolver in its modified holster. A special rivet, which he kept well greased, allowed the holster to swivel effortlessly in a full circle on the belt.

Mastering it required long practice. But by now Frank didn't have to lose that critical fraction of a second required to clear the holster and realign the gun arm to fire. He gained another fraction by filing the gun's trigger down so close there was no slack left to take up. By now Frank knew precisely how to make the altered revolver fire itself, simply by jerking it to a stop. No drawing, no manual firing.

"Just swivel and it shoots," he announced out loud as if lecturing a classroom. "You need that extra edge against the likes of Hickok. He's got the speed of a striking snake."

But his unique pistol rig was only the beginning. A man who took a bull by the horns needed more than one way to throw it down. A hidebound chest in the corner contained all of Frank's worldly possessions—including a few more surprises for Hickok.

Frank felt a little better by now. He decided another bottle of Old Crow would whet his appetite for a steak. Not bothering to bathe or shave, he put on his only clean shirt and trousers, then tugged on his scuffed-leather boots, their heels extra high to hold stirrups. Finally he strapped on his shell belt.

Frank Tutt took three flights of carpeted stairs to the big front lobby. It was a slow afternoon, and the lobby was nearly deserted. Just several proper ladies in ostrich-feather hats and rustling bustles. They shared a circular sofa while they exclaimed over the latest Montgomery Ward catalog.

Frank stepped out onto the raw-lumber boardwalk for a breath of fresh air before he started drinking again. It was a hot, sunny, windless day, the white dome of the new opera house next door gleaming like marble in the late-afternoon sun.

The Depression of '73 had left much of the nation destitute and cash-starved. But Santa Fe remained a frontier oasis and boomtown, prosperous as a pretty whore at end-of-tracks. Signs all over the city advertised HELP WANTED, some of them adding in parentheses: ORPHANS PREFERRED.

"Sons of bitches," Frank said out loud to no one in particular. " 'Round here, you all got money to throw at the birds, ain'tcha's? Well, kiss my lily-white ass. I'll take what I need, and you'll smile while I do it."

Truth was, he hated this damned mongrel town. All the Mex and gringo customs got all mixed up, so's a man got them damned tortillas with his eggs instead of biscuits.

Frank stood there stretching out the hangover kinks. A yellow boil of dust rolled toward him as a half-dozen cowboys pushed a small herd through town. Some of the brindled longhorns had horns spreading up to seven feet.

Frank watched the yipping, weather-rawed cowboys and felt contempt for all those proud, dirt-poor men. Buncha damned cow nurses! He'd tried it himself once, out in west Texas. Thirty a month and grub, you furnish your own rig and bedroll. Call that living? Hell, even a sheep-herder's wages were double that. But pretty damn quick now, Frank Tutt, too, would have money to throw at the birds. Ten thousand dollars, to be exact. The price on Hickok's head.

Frank headed back inside the hotel and crossed the lobby toward the adjoining saloon. He thought about the little surprise he'd left on the trail for Hickok and his pard. Unless somebody else reached it first, they should be riding into it any old time now. Just a little clue so that Hickok would start worrying.

"Excuse me, Mr. Tutt?"

Frank snapped his head around toward the

front desk. A bald headed clerk wearing sleeve garters waved him over.

"Mr. Tutt, I noticed on your registration card that you put down 'vermin exterminator' as your occupation?"

Frank grinned. It was a private joke. "That's right. Why?"

The clerk pointed toward the nearest corner. The front half of a long, black rat protruded from a hole, sniffing the air for a food scent.

"There it is again, Mr. Tutt. Bold as a harlot! That damned rat's been plaguing us for a month now. You can well imagine how painful that is to those of us who take pride in the Dorsey's reputation."

"Why, sure. Fine place like this."

"Exactly. Sir, would you recommend strychnine or mercury poison to kill a rat?"

"Here's what I recommend for rats. Two-legged or four."

Frank tapped the butt of his Navy Colt with the heel of his palm, swiveling his riveted holster around into firing position without drawing the gun. He had practiced shooting this way from the hip for years.

He didn't touch the filed-down trigger—the simple, sudden force of stopping the gun's movement released the hammer. A .38-caliber slug blew the rat into several bloody chunks. One of the women screamed and swooned. The clerk turned pale as new linen. The acrid stink of burnt saltpeter filled the lobby.

"Would the service I just rendered," Frank asked the astounded clerk, "be worth another day's lodging?"

"Two days," the visibly impressed clerk hastened to assure him. "With laundry service tossed in."

Chapter Two

Joshua was still too busy, gloating and taunting Wild Bill, to notice how Old Smoke had drifted right over to the edge of a vast prickly-pear patch.

"I've read that some of your best bronc-peelers," Josh boasted over his shoulder, "grew up in big cities back east just like I did. Ace Parker out of New York City, Bo Simmons out of Boston, Sammy 'Leather Butt' Levinski out of Cincinnati."

"Uh-huh," Bill responded with a serious expression. "And now Josh Robinson out of Philly."

"You know, Wild Bill? I still got my last remittance payment from my editor. Now that I'm a horseman, I'm buying chaps and spurs when we hit Santa Fe!"

"Yeah, kid," Bill said quietly as he watched the fading day, which seemed to watch him back

22

from the eyes of a sullen animal. "You're definitely the big he-bear hereabouts."

Bill couldn't believe it. The journalist was so full of himself he hadn't even noticed yet how loose his saddle cinch was—Old Smoke was slyly holding his stomach distended to steady it. But all that was about to change.

"Would you recommend angora chaps or leather?" Josh demanded.

"Depends where you wear 'em. Angora's for cold winters. Leather's for cactus."

"Sure," the kid responded, as if he'd known that all along. "Well, should I get star-roweled spurs like yours, Bill? With the five points? You know, there's some that swear by three points . . ."

Josh was still nattering on in this vein when Old Smoke made his move. The agile mustang sprang straight up and jackknifed its spine quick to upset the rider's balance. Then he gave a shuddering twist in midair designed to toss Josh off on the right-hand side.

Old Smoke's treachery worked perfectly. The loose saddle whipped round to the right like a tent in a tornado. Josh catapulted out of the stirrups head over handcart. He landed, hind end first, on a spiked mound of prickly pear.

The yowl of pain Josh loosed made Bill feel a moment of guilt for not warning him. But how many times had he tried to tell the kid to keep his head screwed on straight? The soft-brained city dweller had to learn the high price of cockiness on the frontier.

"Don't move," Bill called out to the grimacing, howling newspaperman. "I'll reel you in."

Bill swung down, a man of medium height and build, lithe and muscled. He hobbled his horse foreleg to rear, then caught the gray's halter and hobbled it, too. Then he took the lariat off Josh's saddle horn and shook out a few coils.

"Grab the end, kid, and just hand-walk your way out."

Bill flicked his wrist, and the end of the rope snapped out toward the tail-hooked kid. Josh, still yowling like a butt-shot dog, caught the rope. Bill braced himself, and the youth pulled himself up gingerly, hand over hand.

"My ass is on fire," he wailed, limping pathetically. "Katy Christ, Bill! Feels like a thousand red ants are biting at once!"

Bill slid a case knife out of his left saddle pocket and pried out the smallest blade.

"Kid, you're alla time scribbling down notes. So write this down, too. It's an old cowboy rhyme from the Brasada country: 'There ain't no hoss that can't be rode; there ain't no man that can't be throwed.' Now shuck down your trousers and drawers. Those barbs will have to be cut outta you one by one."

"Cut?"

"What, we got an echo? Damn it, kid, hurry up, wouldja? We're burning good daylight."

"That animal is *laughing*," Josh said bitterly as he unlooped his suspenders. "Look at him, Bill."

Indeed, Old Smoke's lips were drawn away from his teeth. As the horse watched Josh, its sturdy frame seemed to shake with silent mirth.

Bill said, "He knows a fool when he sees one, that's why. Now hold still, Longfellow. I ain't got all day to play peekaboo with your sitter. I mean to sleep under a roof tonight in Chimayo."

Ten minutes later, Bill tossed the moaning Josh a bottle of calomel lotion. "I'm damned if I'm rubbing it on for you. Hurry up, we gotta make tracks."

Josh watched Bill reach up and place his hand between the sun and the horizon.

" 'Bout four fingers left," Bill announced. "That means only about a half hour of good daylight."

Josh reset his saddle, careful of the girth this time. They hit the trail again, following a long ascent up a creosote ridge. At the top, despite their hurry, Bill and Josh pulled in so their horses could blow.

"There's Chimayo," Bill said, pointing to a tight cluster of adobe buildings down below in a fertile valley. Wild columbine colored the surrounding pastures and meadows with splashes of sky blue. Why, Bill wondered, was no one working in the *milpas*, the communal fields?

"Too damn much of the land is under fence now," Bill complained just before they rode on. "I pushed stagecoaches through the West when you couldn't find one fence between El Paso and Bozeman. The free-range days are over."

Josh stood up in the stirrups to ease the pressure on his thorn-ravaged rear end. Bill shook his head in disgust.

"Kid, if your antlers were any greener, they'd be Christmas trees. Did *I* teach you that stupid trick?"

"What stupid trick?" Josh demanded.

"Skylining yourself like that on a ridge in open country. Why'n't you just yell 'gobble gobble' at a turkey shoot, you young fool?"

Josh flushed. Wincing at the pain, he lowered himself gingerly into the saddle again. "Yeah, that's right."

"Fresh off ma's milk," Bill said as he nudged his horse forward. "Suffer the little children."

Josh knew Bill wasn't really all that mad at him. Usually Hickok viewed Josh's shoddy trailcraft with mild good humor. But he always became snappish when he ran out of cigars and bourbon. However, as they descended nearer to the village, they soon realized they had bigger troubles than a shortage of luxuries.

The few dwellings were of puddled adobe, the Indian style, with layers of grass-impregnated mud poured between forms, drying one layer on another. Even this poor excuse for a village had its solid adobe church with thick, buttressed walls. But the town seemed like a graveyard. At first they noticed no one, and the only sound came from an old, rotting windlass creaking like a rusty hinge in the breeze.

"Man alive," Josh said nervously. "What's going on around here, Wild Bill?"

"Not too damn much, huh?"

Hickok's gunmetal-blue eyes closed to a squint in the setting sun. The two riders slowed their horses from a trot to a walk. Bill noticed bright prayer plumes planted in front of some of the houses—only planted in times of duress to seek special mercy from the *indio* gods. That puzzled Bill. Chimayo was a mix of Mexicans and Indians, but had long been a solidly Catholic village.

"There! There's some people."

Josh pointed behind the church.

Bill followed the kid's finger. About two dozen Pueblo Indians—men, women, and children—were gathered in an irrigation ditch. They were scrubbing themselves with yucca root, which created a rich, white lather.

"They must like being clean," Josh commented. "They're sure scrubbing hard enough."

"They ain't scrubbing off dirt," Bill replied grimly. He had just spotted something else. He pointed it out for Josh—a white towel had been tied to a stake in front of the nearest house.

"What's that?" Josh demanded. "Who they surrendering to?"

"Nobody. It's a warning. The town's under epidemic. Probably either smallpox or the black-rat plague. That towel warns strangers to keep riding. As for that bunch . . ."

Bill nodded toward the irrigation ditch again. "Indians around here scrub with yucca root when they want to wash away unclean influences. Like white man's baptism. See how the church is closed up? I'd wager these Indians think they're being punished by their old gods for praying to new gods."

"That might be why they're staring at us so hard," Josh speculated. "They don't look too happy to see us."

"Nope. We best keep riding. I know another spot near here with water and graze. Called Chico Springs. It's a campsite for wagon trains after they round Point of Rocks on the Cimarron Cutoff."

Their hoofclops echoed eerily as they rode through the nearly deserted village. Yellow plumes of dust rose behind them, floating a long time in the hot, still air. Bill's eyes, shaded under his hat, stayed in constant motion, noticing the best ambush points.

"Jehoshaphat!"

The journalist flinched at a sudden darting motion in the corner of his eye. But it was only a tumbleweed, rolling on a sudden, hot gust of wind. It was the only plant Josh knew of that didn't put down roots, but instead roamed in search of water.

At the far edge of town, an old Indian woman wrapped in a dark rebozo sat cross-legged in front of her hovel. She was crushing corn on a metate, a grinding stone. Using an odd mix of Spanish and English, known as Spanglish throughout the border region, Bill managed to purchase two wooden bowls of cornmeal gruel.

The old *abuela* seemed grateful for the fifty cents in silver dimes Bill generously paid her. But she avoided their eyes, and politely but firmly ignored Bill's attempts at conversation. She seemed relieved when they finished eating and slipped the hobbles from their horses.

"Oye, abuela," Bill said to the old woman as he swung up and over, reining his horse around. "What's going on here? Why are you so scared?"

For a long moment, she pretended to ignore the questions. Finally the old woman's frightened, coffee-colored eyes peered out from under her shawl.

"Hidalgo," she responded in a cracked and sere old voice. She made the sign of the cross. *"Afuera!"* she added, gesturing wildly. *"Afuera!* Get out now while you can! The Curse of Hidalgo is on all of us! We who live here are as good as dead!"

Josh's instincts as a newspaperman told him to stay in Chimayo and ferret out the story of this terror-stricken pueblo. The AP might telegraph his dispatch to every major newspaper in the country. Especially if Wild Bill was prominently mentioned.

But those were professional instincts. His instincts as a badly outnumbered white man made him feel relieved to get the hell out of town.

There was little sunlight left now, and Hickok set a fast pace to take advantage of what remained. He and Josh had split the remuda, so each man had two horses following on a lead line. Santa Fe still lay well to the south of them, another full day's ride. So Bill led them due east off the Santa Fe Trail, hoping to make Chico Springs by nightfall or just past.

The riding, even on the narrow old trace Bill now took, was mostly easy while light held out. Although jagged mountains surrounded them on the distant horizons, up close the terrain was mostly gentle scrubhills dotted with creosote and cholla. Despite the peacefulness of it all, however, Josh couldn't shake the image of the old grandmother's terrified eyes. Whatever the "Curse of Hidalgo" was, it had an entire town under its evil thrall.

Wild Bill led them due east, showing amazing memory of the country for a man who hadn't ridden these trails since the 1850s. Indeed, like a canny showman, Bill seemed to know exactly which spectacular sights to show Josh—those that would most appeal to millions of avid newspaper readers back in the Land of Steady Habits. Yesterday Bill had showed him where the famous Pecos River rises in the Sangre de Cristo mountains before twisting and rioting southward to plague cowboys and smugglers alike.

All this rolled through Josh's thoughts. Bill had to raise his voice to get the youth's attention.

"Damn it, kid, you think I love my own voice? Save the dreaming until you're asleep. I said pull in and check your rig. We got a long, steep slope ahead before we hit the springs. It'll be hard to stop if your saddle slips again."

Josh flushed angrily at himself for being so ten-derfooted even after almost a year sidekicking with Wild Bill. That was twice now Bill had to remind him they were riding through outlaw country, not dancing on Fiddler's Green. Yelping at the pain in his butt, the youth swung down to reset his saddle and check the cinch and latigos.

"This ain't a particularly hard ride," Bill said, nodding toward the slope out ahead. "Not for a peeler like you."

Bill's grin was so good-natured, Josh had to join him.

"Stick close to the trail, you'll be all right," Bill assured him. "Just stay behind me. Hold tight rein, but let Old Smoke set his own pace. It turns a little steep toward the bottom is all, and your horse might have to slide the last few yards. Full moon and plenty of stars, so we'll be all right."

Josh felt a tickle in his stomach as he stepped up into leather again and took up the slack in his reins. Old Smoke had settled down since tossing Josh into the cactus patch earlier today. But the slope stretching out before them in the silvery moonlight looked mighty long and steep.

Bill, who only used spurs in a shooting scrape, started the white mustang forward with a squeeze of his legs. Both animals, like all the remounts, had spent their early lives in the high sierras of

Sonora. They handled the descending slope with the surefootedness of mules and bighorn sheep.

"Why, it's a Sunday picnic!" Josh called ahead to Wild Bill, starting to enjoy the excitment of this wild plunge.

A few moments after Josh spoke, however, the slope grew noticeably steeper. He hugged the gray's neck, hunkering lower in the saddle to keep from sliding off forward.

Thank goodness Wild Bill's pure white mare was easy to keep an eye on so that Josh could hold the narrow trail. Tall, thin cactus plants, called Spanish bayonets by the local Indians, began to crowd the trail on both sides. A careless rider could get skinned alive—and Josh wanted no more run-ins with cactus.

Suddenly, even as Josh watched, Bill's horse just dropped out from under Hickok—literally swallowed up by the earth.

Wild Bill, thanks in part to his early days as a Pony Express rider, was famous for quick horse-back thinking. Even as he felt his mount drop, Hickok lifted both feet from the stirrups, planted them on his saddle pommel, and kicked upward with a mighty flexing of his strong legs. One hand still gripped the lead line holding his remounts.

Josh barely managed to rein left and avoid the trouble spot himself. He gaped in even greater astonishment at what happened next: As Bill's mount disappeared, Hickok managed to land on the bare back of his favorite, the chestnut with the roached mane.

Josh heard a piteous cry of pain from the white mustang, pain that came from deep wounds. Then he and Bill got caught in a confused, sliding rush of whickering animals and boiling dust and

31

chunks of loose scree. Moments later, they reached a grassy flat at the bottom of the slope, a sliding but safe landing.

"God Almighty!" Josh exclaimed. The shrieking horse could still be heard above them, making enough racket to wake snakes. "What in Sam Hill happened, Bill?"

"Pitfall trap," Bill replied tersely. "Well made, too. Hobble your horse, kid, and follow me. Keep an eye peeled."

"Indians do it?" Josh demanded, scrambling up the slope behind Bill.

"Apaches like a pitfall," Bill replied, his breathing growing more ragged as he fought the slope. "And I've talked to Texas Rangers who say Comanches will rig one now and then, too. But the Comanches are mostly up in Oklahoma now, selling stories to your peers for drinks. The Apaches, I've heard, are mostly out in Arizona or hiding down in Old Mex."

Bill's injured horse, obviously in death agonies, cried out again, the sound reminiscent of a helpless child crying.

"Aw, Christ," Bill muttered in a tone Josh rarely heard him use. It was one of the few sounds Bill could not get used to during the long years of civil war—wounded horses crying. The sound raised a man's fine hairs even more than the noise of human suffering. Bill had watched it literally drive strong men into insane frenzies.

"Good heart of God," Josh murmured when both men reached the deep pitfall. Plenty of moonlight showed the grisly scene.

The dying horse was impaled through its belly and intestines on a wooden stake that had been sharpened to a lethal point and driven deep into the ground. Cursing softly, Bill drew one of his pearl-gripped Colt .44s and immediately shot the suffering animal in the head.

"Damn it, kid," Bill said, his eyes searching the moonlit slope all around them. "That animal had bony withers. But she also had good bottom and always bucked to the same pattern. She was a good animal, and didn't deserve that."

"Why would Indians do this?" Josh wondered. "I thought they respected horses?"

"Apaches damn sure respect horses—it's their favorite meat. But Indians didn't do this."

"How can you know that?"

"And you call yourself a newspaperman? Look there—you tell me what tribe uses a double-hitch knot."

Bill meant the now-broken cover of woven branches that had been placed over the pitfall. They had been tied together with well-knotted ropes.

"That rope, too," Bill added. "It's hemp. White man's rope. Indians around here would use sisal or buffalo hair."

"Well, whoever did it, what could be the point?"

Bill didn't answer. Something inside the pitfall caught his eye. Hickok folded to his knees. Josh watched him reach around the dead mustang. A piece of broken board lay in the bottom of the pit. Bill pulled it out, then stared at it in the moonlight.

"What is it?" Josh demanded.

Bill shook his head. He handed the scrap of wood to the youth. Now Josh saw that the number 18 had been scrawled on the wood with charcoal. Nothing else.

"What's eighteen mean?" Josh asked.

"Christ, kid. It means one more than seventeen, one less than nineteen."

"No, I mean—"

"How the hell would I know what it means? I can't find sign in tea leaves. Hell, maybe it don't mean a damn thing."

Bill again studied the surrounding terrain.

"Well," he said finally, "let's get below and make camp for the night. Much as I hate to, we better take turns on guard."

"Bill?" Josh said as the two men trudged down the slope.

"Yeah?"

"That trap . . . it wasn't dug deliberately for us, was it? You, I mean."

"I don't see how. Nobody knows I'm heading this way."

"And why the number eighteen? Is that—"

"Kid, give it a rest, wouldja?" Bill snapped. "I came south to have some fun. And damn it all anyway, that's what I mean to do. Even if somebody has to get killed."

Bill fell silent, and a coyote howled from a ridge or two over. Its long, ululating howl ended in a series of yipping barks. The mournful sound, in that windswept vastness, made the hair on Josh's nape stiffen.

"Fun," Bill repeated defiantly. But the night only mocked him in silence.

Chapter Three

Frank Tutt slept off his hangover and woke up late on his second afternoon in Santa Fe, feeling fit as a rutting buck. He bathed and shaved, then visited the hotel dining room and ordered himself a steak with all the trimmings.

A quick check with a porter at the nearby La Fonda Hotel revealed that Hickok had not yet checked in. If he didn't reach town by sundown, Frank decided, that meant there was a good chance he was hurt or killed by the pitfall Frank had dug near Chico Springs.

But Frank did not, as had so many of J. B. Hickok's vanquished foes, underestimate Wild Bill's survival skills. He knew Hickok would probably head for Chico Springs—with Chimayo under plague, it was the nearest graze and water. But mainly, that trap was an opportunity to leave a clue for Hickok. Tell him, but *not* tell him. After all, what good was revenge if a man couldn't enjoy it?

No, Frank reminded himself as he returned to his room at the Dorsey. Before he moved in for the actual kill, eyeball to eyeball, he would let Hickok know what was happening. When you gun down a Tutt, then by God you'd best kill 'em *all*.

Frank crossed to the hidebound chest in the corner and opened it with a key he kept in his fob pocket. He removed the major groups of a disassembled .56 Spencer carbine, wrapped in clean cloths. This weapon, equipped with the 7x crosshair scope Frank had special-ordered for it, was the highly effective sniping gun of the U.S. Army's new mountain regiments, tasked with killing Indians in their hiding places.

Frank assembled the Spencer but left the scope off for now. He propped the carbine against the wall and finished unpacking the trunk.

Its contents included a rattan walking stick, in two sections that screwed together. A fragment of mirror had been embedded into the curved handle so it could be used to look around corners or into doorways. Frank also removed and inspected his "drinking jewelry"—curved horseshoe nails welded together so they easily slipped over his knuckles in a fistfight. With one straight-arm punch, Frank had once used them in Amarillo to bust seven teeth out of a cowboy's mouth.

But his special arsenal wasn't complete until Frank removed a pair of heavy work boots with gut stitching. The right boot had been ingeniously rigged by a ferrier in St. Louis. Frank tripped a spring near the heel, and five inches of razor-sharp iron blade popped out the front of the thick sole, automatically locking into place. One kick to an opponent's groin could turn a rooster into a capon.

Frank checked the slant of the sun's shadow on the floor. Late afternoon. If Hickok was coming, he'd be here soon. Let the puffed-up, back-shooting bastard come!

A trio of sudden, loud knocks on the door made Frank flinch. He eased his Navy Colt up to the ready, simply rotating the specially riveted holster without needing to draw the long-barreled weapon.

"Who is it?" he demanded.

"Queen Victoria," replied a low, sarcastic voice with a trace of Spanish accent.

Frank hastened to open the door for his boss.

"Wolf," he said, greeting a dark, thin, dangerous-looking man wearing a low shako hat. "I wondered when you'd get here."

The bandit king known throughout the Southwest as El Lobo Flaco—the Skinny Wolf—stepped into the room and crossed to the whiskey bottle on a nightstand beside the bed. He lowered the contents by a few inches. Then he looked at Tutt from small, mud-colored eyes.

"Tell me, Frank," he said in his low, almost whispering voice, "why I should not kill you for deserting your post? I told you to watch the Raton Pass, *verdad?* Night and day."

"Boss, if I 'deserted,' would I send you word where to find me?"

El Lobo never came into town without donning his infamous leggings that struck terror into friend and foe alike. One leg was decorated with the brightly painted whole fingernails of Americans, the other leg with those of *Mexicanos.*

"'*Sta bien*. All right, I am here," El Lobo said impatiently. "And I am a very busy man, Frank. Are we playing guess my secret? Why did you abandon your post?"

"Because I knew you'd want me to. Wild Bill Hickok is on his way to Santa Fe—might be here right now."

El Lobo took manly pride in never showing his emotions. Nonetheless, at this unwelcome news, a shadow moved across his face.

"*Maldito*," he cursed in a whisper. Out loud he demanded, "You are sure it is Hickok?"

Frank snorted. "Sure I'm sure. That skirt-chasing poncy shot my brother in the back."

"But of course you do not know *why* he has come?"

Tutt shook his head. "Not yet. But Hickok likes his fancy ladies. I'd wager he's here to find one of 'em."

"It is probably not because of the bell," El Lobo agreed. "It is too soon for word to have reached him. But if he should become involved, *madre de Dios!* That bell weighs seven hundred and fifty pounds. There is no way to cover our trail as we haul it. Unfortunately, we cannot simply take it straight to Los Cerrillos. Someone may guess the truth. Hickok—whatever he is here for, we must watch him closely."

"That's what I thought you'd say, Wolf. That's why I'm here."

"Even better," El Lobo added in a pointed tone, "if Hickok could have an 'accident' before he can make trouble for us."

"I'm still one step ahead of you. Hickok always stays at La Fonda. I've . . . persuaded a kid, who works at the hotel wash house, that he'd be wise to help me out. That first 'accident' should happen soon after Hickok arrives."

By the time Josh and Wild Bill rode into Santa Fe, Hickok had nearly shaken off the incident the day before at Chico Springs.

"You know, kid," he announced cheerfully as they trotted past El Palacio, also known as the Mud Palace, the oldest government house in the United States, "every rainstorm ain't meant just to get *us* wet. That pitfall at Chico Springs coulda been meant for anybody. Local waddies fighting for their brands, anything. I'm putting it away from my thoughts. We're here to cut loose a little, is all. Damn it all, we *will* have a high old time."

But Josh thought Bill's tone was a little too determined—like a man who needed to convince himself, not others. And Hickok's wary, shaded eyes stayed in constant motion. He watched doorways, alleys; the mostly adobe buildings were plastered white and topped by red tile roofs. Josh had observed Indian women making the clay tiles, forming them on their thighs to ensure uniformity without modern equipment.

The first item of business, as always, was to see to the horses. They rode to the livery barn at the edge of town, stripped their rigging and gear, then turned all five horses loose to drink at the trough in front of the barn.

"Wagon yard's full," Bill remarked. He nodded toward a flotilla of buckboards, buggies, coaches, and dray wagons, all neatly lined up in an open-sided shed. "Plenty of travelers means plenty of card games. I've honed you into a fair poker player, kid. But I got no heart for cleaning out a newspaper poet like you who makes forty dollars

39

a month. You can just be dealer when the stakes climb too high."

Bill's mood was improving by the minute. The two dusty, tired riders placed their saddles on racks in the tack room and hung their bridles and headstalls from Arbuckle's coffee cans nailed to the wall.

"Curry 'em good, *chico*," Bill told the young mozo who assisted the owner. He flipped him four bits American. "Grain 'em all, too, wouldja? Crushed barley, if you got it. Don't stall 'em nights unless it rains."

"We'll need to get your sorrel to a blacksmith," Bill commented as both men rinsed off quickly at the water trough out front.

"Why?"

"You deaf, kid? Can't you hear his shoes clacking when you ride him? I told you before, that means they're loose. They'll have to be pulled and reset."

Bill dunked his head in the water, then shook the drops from his long blond curls. The two men were only getting clean enough so they could enter the La Fonda without trailing dirt on the fancy Oriental rugs.

From the livery, it was only a short walk to Santa Fe's oldest and best hotel. This was Josh's first trip to Santa Fe, and the young reporter stood gawking like a rube at his first sight of La Fonda's elegant lobby.

The hand-hewn hemlock beams had been transported cross-country from Pennsylvania. A magnificent carved cherrywood staircase rose in a dizzying spiral toward a walnut cathedral ceiling aglitter with crystal chandeliers. Canaries in gilt cages sent up a melodious chorus.

"Man alive!" Josh marveled, his eyes wide to

take all of it in. "This is the frontier? It looks like Napoleon's palace."

"Palatial" was a good word for it, especially in light of the truly royal reception Wild Bill was given despite his dusty trail clothes. A familiar and famous face at the hotel, Hickok was recognized immediately by the staff. Two lads in fancy livery had a quick scuffle over who got to carry Hickok's saddlebags.

"Touch you for luck, Bill?" demanded an awestruck clerk behind the wide mahogany counter. Bill gave him a hearty handshake. The manager himself emerged from his office behind the counter, holding a copy of Ned Buntline's wildly popular dime novel *Wild Bill, Indian Fighter*. Bill autographed it for him. It amazed, and impressed, Josh when the manager thanked him as if Bill had given him a piece of the cross that bore Christ.

Bill earned this, Josh thought. But I helped it along, too. Brave deeds meet vivid words, and from that happy marriage fame is born. And the serious trouble starts.

While all this fuss went on, Josh gazed around the sumptuously appointed lobby. As he would write later, when he filed his next story from the Western Union office, the La Fonda was a living catalog of the "better" society in the New Mexico Territory of the 1870s.

A group of elegantly dressed young ladies shared a huge circular sofa with a central headrest. They had obviously just detrained—one of them was complaining bitterly about cinder holes in her new silk taffeta gown. At nearby reading tables with green-shaded gas lamps, their fashionably dressed husbands and fathers smoked cigars and commented on stories in the country's major newspapers. Few of them deigned to notice the dusty new arrivals or how deferential the staff was being to them.

Josh, too, was treated like royalty after Bill mentioned he was a reporter for the *New York Herald*. He and Bill were assigned adjoining luxury suites on the second floor. The splendor of the main lobby continued up here. Josh gawped at the gold-gilt mirrors, at fireplaces manteled and faced with blood onyx, marble, and slate. Near the head of a huge *lit du roi* bed was a fancy velvet pull-rope for summoning a bell boy.

"President Grant couldn't have it finer!" Josh exclaimed.

"No more grits and hominy for us, Longfellow," Hickok gloated as he skinned the wrapper off a fancy five-cent cigar the manager had slipped into his pocket. "For the next week or so, we're going to live like young rahjahs. C'mon, there's a good wash house out back. Even got 'em one of the new hot-water boilers. We'll soak in by-God style."

Rooms at La Fonda included toilets and running water, but only cold. Both men grabbed a clean change of clothes, locked their rooms, and headed out back. Josh noticed that Bill obviously knew the La Fonda well—he led the way down a back corridor, even using a service stairwell. Thus, even as word spread that Hickok was staying at the hotel, Bill avoided most of the thrill-seekers and troublemakers.

A Chinese kid in a floppy blue blouse, a few years younger than Josh, was tending the men's half of the wash house. Huge, claw-footed iron tubs were divided by flock-board partitions. A big brass-trimmed hot-water boiler filled one corner.

Every now and then, a safety valve on top the boiler released a jet of hissing steam into a vent in the ceiling.

Hot water at the turn of a spigot was still a comparative luxury on the frontier. But it came with great danger. The technology was still new, and exploding water boilers and steam engines were among the young nation's leading causes of accidental deaths.

Hickok, like most literate folks, read the newspapers, and he knew all this. But he was also the most popular gun target in America. Bill had perfected the art of covering his back. And when his time finally came, he fully expected a bullet to do the deed—not some mundane mishap that killed clerks and preachers.

Thus, Bill paid little attention when the Chinese kid, his hair braided into a two-foot pigtail, led him to the tub right next to the boiler. In fact, Bill preferred this spot for security reasons. It put the huge iron boiler behind him while leaving a good view of the entire building.

The kid filled the adjacent tub for Joshua. Then he gave both men clean towels and little cakes of fancy French soap—not yellow lumps of lye-and-ash soap used most places. Then he excused himself, bowing before he hauled out a bag bulging with dirty towels intended for the laundry.

Bill had already sent a bellboy to fetch him a bottle of Old Taylor bourbon. Hickok stuck the nickel stogy between his teeth, placed the bourbon near the tub, and began whistling cheerfully as he stripped. Bill removed the long gray duster that did double duty: It protected his clothing (for Hickok was notoriously fastidious about his

43

appearance), and it hid the distinctive, fancy pearl grips of his Colt .44s.

The water boiler thumped and clanged. Bill paid little heed, wincing as he eased his bare flesh into the water. Hickok left both guns within reach beside the bourbon bottle.

"Now, this is more like it, kid."

Bill sighed, placing his stogy aside to duck his head under the water. He shot back up, water running from his head in rivulets.

"We'll scrub up, change, wrap our teeth around some decent grub. After that, guess I'll visit the hotel bar and find myself a high-stakes poker game. Might even cap the night off with a trip to the opera."

The hot-water tank thumped and clanged again. Idly, Josh wondered why the pressure-release valve on top wasn't hissing open. Bill whistled a few cheerful bars of "Buffalo Gal."

"And best of all," he gloated, lifting one arm to scrub under it, "*no* ornery, stinking, ugly, cussing Calamity Jane on our trail. I ain't seen scratch nor hair of her in months, knock on wood. That woman is death to the devil."

Getting mighty warm in here, Josh thought as beads of sweat trickled out of his hairline.

"Bill?"

"Mmm?"

"That business back in Chimayo . . . you ever heard of this Curse of Hidalgo?"

"Nah. But down here, there's more curses than flies. The priests encourage it. They know their flocks will buy extra novenas for their souls. It's sound business—you won't see any skinny priests down here."

"Pretty hot in here," Josh remarked.

"Now, Longfellow," Bill nattered on happily, "don't forget. We ain't joined at the hip. I only mention that so you'll know to dust if I should strike up a likely acquaintance with a member of the fair sex."

"How do you know," Josh demanded, "that *I* won't get lucky first? Plenty of women like me."

Bill laughed. "Hell yes they do. It must be the bowler hat. Or maybe your high-school education. Who *wouldn't* fancy a fellow who writes sentences like 'Wild Bill spends most of his time ducking the ultimate arrow.'"

Josh flushed. The water heater started clanging in earnest, but both men ignored it.

"The ultimate arrow—it's figurative is all. Women admire a man who's good with words," Josh protested.

"Wha'd'ya think I use on 'em, kid, a breaking saddle? Ahh, cheer up. Who knows? This is Santa Fe. We might even find some sweetie in sprigged muslin for you."

Josh opened his mouth to retort. An eyeblink later, all hell broke loose when the water heater exploded.

Only Hickok's razor-honed reflexes saved him from sure decapitation. Just a heartbeat before the front iron plate blew off, shooting only inches above the top of Hickok's tub, the pressure valve popped loose with a sound like a gun discharging. That too-familiar sound immediately sent Hickok diving to the bottom of his wash tub.

The force of the main explosion blew out one section of wall in a comber of steaming water. It also blew both surprised and naked bathers out of their overturned tubs in a sprawling, sudsy confusion.

"God kiss me!" Hickok exclaimed. "You all right, Joshua?"

"I—I think so. Holy Hannah! What happened?"

The place was a shambles, but nobody was hurt. Most of the scalding water blew over them. The two men scrambled into their clothing even as worried hotel employees rushed inside. All, Josh noticed, except the Chinese kid.

"A *terrible* accident, Mr. Hickok," the manager was sputtering even as Bill tucked in his shirttail. "My profuse apologies."

"Accidents happen," Bill assured him, dismissing the incident in his usual quiet, gentlemanly manner. But Josh noticed how Bill, too, was looking around for that Chinese kid.

Always nervous in any crowd, Hickok slipped back to his room on the second floor, Josh following him. The youth was about to key his lock when he noticed Wild Bill staring at his own door, motionless as a statue of salt.

Josh moved a few steps to glance over Hickok's shoulder. Abruptly, the youth felt his scalp tingling as if lice were crawling all over it.

Someone had written, evidently with charcoal, the number 65 just above the fancy glass knob of Bill's door. Josh immediately thought of that board they'd found in the pitfall at Chico Springs. It had an 18 on it, also in charcoal. But what did the numbers mean?

The two men locked gazes.

"Kid," Bill said, his tone weary, "am I a trouble-seeking man by nature?"

Josh shook his head. "You kidding? You go out of your way to avoid it."

"The way you say. But trouble always makes a

point of looking me up. That pitfall wasn't just there by happenchance, kid. And that explosion just now was accidental-on-purpose. Keep a weather eye out. We've walked into a stacked deck, and so far it's dealer's game."

Chapter Four

"I don't get it," Josh pestered while Wild Bill fussed over himself in the mirror. "First the number eighteen, then the number sixty-five. What does it mean? The year 1865?"

Hickok continued to carefully comb out his blond mustache. "Who knows?" he replied with little interest. "Who teaches little kids to play hopscotch? Look. I told you, Longfellow, we are not—repeat *not*—here in Santa Fe so you can get a good story."

Wild Bill wore a dark suit of worsted wool with a silk-lined vest and an octagon tie. Josh, too, was all spruced up, his pomaded hair slick and shiny as a new saddle.

"Yeah? Well, whoever rigged that boiler to blow up seems to have different plans for you," the young reporter said. "I still say we should find that Chinese kid. You notice how he disappeared right before the explosion?"

"I'll talk to him," Bill said, slapping bay rum tonic on his fresh-shaven cheeks. "The manager thinks the pressure-release valve got stuck."

"Is that what you think, too?"

"Oh, it got stuck all right," Bill agreed, frustrating Josh with his cryptic answer.

"Eighteen and sixty-five. Could it mean the year 1865?" Josh repeated.

"Couldn't tell you, kid," Bill replied as he strapped on his leather gunbelt. He pulled each Colt from its hand-tooled holster to palm the wheel, checking his loads.

"You don't seem too worried about it, either," Josh pointed out.

"I didn't ride all the way down here to worry. Kid, why should I work up a brain sweat? Face the facts. While sheriff in Abilene, I killed a man who needed killing. Texan named Lofley. His old man is a cattle baron. So now there's a ten-thousand-dollar bounty on me, payable to the hombre who delivers my head to old man Lofley. With all the jaspers who're trying to kill me, why should I waste time looking for them? Does a man give up on the entire day just because he might have to fight for one minute of it?"

A hotel valet delivered Bill's freshly brushed hat. He clapped it on. "Let's head downstairs," he added, "and scare up a poker game. Since your ma's Quaker, you can take over dealing when the stakes get sinfully high."

Josh followed Hickok down the spiraling central staircase, feeling a nervousness stirring in his belly. He'd seen Hickok like this before. Once the famed frontiersman decided to cut the wolf loose a bit, everything else ceased to matter until his wild oats were sown.

Thus, Josh, too, was armed tonight. Nearly a year ago, when Josh first met him in Denver, Bill had given him an old, but well-maintained, LeFaucheux six-shot pinfire revolver. The ornately detailed French firearm was beautiful and even included a foldaway knife blade under the barrel. Now Josh wore the gun in a chamois holster under his left armpit. Thank God he could shoot better than he could ride, thanks to Bill's tutelage.

The youth from Philadelphia soon realized why Wild Bill enjoyed returning to Santa Fe and the Hotel La Fonda—he was treated like virtual royalty in the New Mexico Territory. Indeed, Hickok was soon "holding court" in the vast hotel barroom, the grand attraction of the night. Everyone, from weather-rawed cowboys to wealthy cattle buyers, made a point of stopping by his table to "touch him for luck." Several bottles of Old Taylor, each label signed by Colonel Taylor himself, appeared at Bill's elbow.

Hickok remained polite and genial with all comers. But Josh could tell Wild Bill was in the mood for romantic intrigue. Rules of propriety were more relaxed in scandalous Santa Fe, where even "proper" women sometimes smoked and imbibed liquor in public establishments. It was these females Hickok kept an eye out for. And Josh noticed they were watching the handsome legend right back. From dime-a-dance girls to elegant opera stars in ostrich-feather boas.

He always gets his pick of the litter, Josh thought with a sting of jealousy. *The ladies don't even see*

*any other man, as if his shadow obscures them.
And it's writers like me who've created the Wild Bill
mystique in the first place.*

Thus wallowing in self-pity, Josh failed to notice when a big, sandy-haired man, wearing fancy oxblood boots and a well-tailored gray suit, made his way closer to the table where Josh sat playing five-card draw with Bill. Two other well-dressed players had joined them.

"Hickok, you son of a bitch! You're a low-down, horse-stealing, barn-burning, skirt-chasing, card-cheating prissy yahoo. I'll make you wear your ass for a hat, you scurvy-infested Irish sot! Or maybe I'll just plug you right now and cash in your female curls for Texas money."

The barroom went silent like a classroom after a tough question. Josh, who was dealing, laid the deck aside. The big man stepped even closer, and the crowd parted like water before the prow of a ship. Josh heard chairs scuff the floor as folks cleared a ballistics lane.

Bill calmly mulled his cards, a slim cheroot stuck between his teeth.

"Joshua," he said, and in that quiet hush his voice carried without effort. "I ever tell you about a poker genius named Mitt McGinnis? Ugly as a pus sore, and the man would steal dead flies from a blind spider. But he was also the best cattleman anywhere near Abilene. The man taught me a valuable rule of poker etiquette: *Never* clean a man out at cards. You should always leave him burying money as a courtesy."

Laughter bubbled through the barroom. The tension eased like a fist relaxing.

The new arrival raised a jolt glass of amber whiskey high over his head.

"Ladies and gentlemen! A moment of your time, please! Most of you know me. I've been whipping beeves on the butt—excuse me, ladies—since I was a little shaver. Some call me a rich cattleman, though I'm no Rockefeller. But back in '71, up in Abilene, Kansas, I stood to lose every red cent I owned. All of us up there did. Banks, trains, coaches, nothing nor no one was safe from outlaws. Gunsels like Stoney MacGruder and Reno Sloan, men that would kill you for your boots."

McGinnis paused to nod toward Hickok's table.

"But in 1871, James Butler Hickok was hired on as marshal of Abilene. Cost us a hundred and fifty dollars a month to get him, if you can believe that."

A murmur of surprise rolled through the crowd.

"Well, he was worth ten times that! He brought such ironfisted justice with him that not *one dollar* was stolen during his tenure."

"Except by you, Mitt, at the card table," Bill quipped wryly before he tasted his bourbon. "This man marks the aces with cigar ashes." More laughter rippled through the barroom.

"Thanks to that perfumed dandy's single-handed courage," McGinnis went on in a burst of heartfelt eloquence, "any hardcases who survived left Abilene wiser if not better men. And that let me and many other westering folk get our start. So ladies and gentlemen, a toast!"

Now Mitt's voice was completely sincere.

"To Wild Bill Hickok! He's one man, armed with skill and raw courage. And he's held all the lawless elements at bay in the toughest towns on the frontier. Here's to a *man*!"

Cheers and applause exploded like a thunderclap.

"Hear, hear!" someone shouted enthusiastically. "To Wild Bill!"

More cheering and clapping. In that heady moment, Josh felt ashamed of the petty jealousy he'd felt just minutes before. This well-spoken Mitt McGinnis was dead right. Hickok *did* do those things, and more. Josh was proud to be sitting beside him—even if the arrogant dandy did order him around like a personal valet.

"Well, Mitt?" Wild Bill asked his old friend when the hubbub died down. "You gonna stand there blubbering and slopping over all night? Or you gonna let me lighten your wallet?"

"Money in my pocket," the wealthy cattle buyer boasted. "But say, Bill. My kid sister Liddy is with me—she's visiting from St. Louis. That's her sipping lemonade over by the doors—see her in the ribboned hat? May she join us?"

Josh glanced up from his cards and looked where McGinnis pointed. A strikingly pretty young woman with ash-blond hair gazed curiously around the room, fascinated but also a little intimidated by this exuberant crush of southwestern society. Women from good families were smoking little dark Mexican cigarettes—and exposing so much of their nearly bare breasts that some might as well have been naked!

"Ladies are always welcome, Mitt," Bill said without bothering to look up from his cards. "This is Santa Fe, not Hays City. Gents, watch your language and don't spit or scratch yourselves in front of her."

Mitt McGinnis left and returned, leading a tall, slender woman wearing a white silk dress with a bertha of point lace. Her pretty, fine-boned face was lightly dusted with powder. All the men stood up at her arrival. Now, Josh noticed, Bill was indeed paying attention.

Mitt obviously doted on his kid sister. He installed her in a chair between Josh and Wild Bill. After brief introductions all around, the game went forward, Josh dealing, Liddy observing. She cast several slanted glances at Wild Bill.

"You know, Miss McGinnis," Hickok said politely as he tossed down two discards, "La Fonda serves an excellent claret. Shall I order you a glass?"

"You're not getting *my* sister drunk, you rascal," Mitt chimed in. "She's a lass of virtue—an aberration, in my family."

"I'd love a glass of claret, Mr. Hickok, thank you," Liddy said defiantly—*in a voice like waltzing violins,* thought the admiring Josh. "From everything I've read or heard about Wild Bill, he's a gentleman above all else. A lady's virtue is safe around him."

Sure, thought Josh. *Because he doesn't need to rob what they surrender willingly.* He watched Bill and Liddy exchange a private little smile. Josh smarted with jealousy.

Thus the night progressed. Bill's legendary luck held this evening. He took trick after trick, and soon gold coins glittered in front of him on the green-baize surface of the table. But even as Hickok's winnings piled up, he managed to engage Liddy in increasingly flirtatious banter. She gave as good as she got. A second glass of claret helped things along.

Only Josh, who knew him well by now, realized how vigilant Wild Bill remained even as poker, alcohol, and the hyacinth fragrance of a lovely woman vied for his attention.

He hadn't forgotten that "accident" in the wash house. Early on, Bill had selected a chair with solid wall behind it and a good view of the big barroom. He closely scrutinized anyone who neared the table. And despite his relaxed posture, both pearl-gripped .44s remained close to hand.

"Bill," Mitt interjected at one point, "I know you're camped here in the hotel. But you'll have to visit my spread, the Lazy M. Plenty of room for you and your friend. Wait till you see how I'm branching out. Besides raising beeves, I'm breeding and training camels for the U.S. Army. The Lazy M is only ten miles south of town on the road to Pecos. We've got the fancy carriage tonight—why don't you and young Joshua here come on back with us?"

Bill aimed a gunmetal gaze at Liddy; her cornflower-blue eyes looked demurely away. But clearly, thought an envious Josh, it was a come-hither gesture.

"We'd be honored," Bill replied, still watching Liddy.

His first night in town, Josh thought bitterly. And another fresh flower is as good as plucked.

However, Hickok's moment of triumph was brief.

A few more minutes passed, Bill and Liddy flirting shamelessly. She had progressed to calling him "Bill" rather than Mr. Hickok. Abruptly, a young Mexican boy about ten or twelve years old stopped at the table.

"Señor Wild Bill?"

"That's me."

"*Perdón.* My mistress, La Señorita Elena Vargas, told me to deliver this to you. *Es muy importante.*"

The kid handed Hickok a folded sheet of fancy, deckle-edged stationery.

"Elena Vargas," Mitt repeated, adding a whistle to show he was impressed. "That gal's rolling in it. And she's easy to look at, too."

Even from where he sat, Josh could smell the expensive perfume. Hickok broke the wax seal and read the brief message. His blond eyebrows met when he frowned.

"Señor? My mistress told me I must wait for your reply."

"Tell her," Bill finally answered, "that I'll be right there."

Hickok looked at Mitt, then at his frowning sister.

"Sorry. Something's come up. We won't be able to visit the Lazy M tonight."

Josh looked at Liddy's slightly puffy, heart-shaped lips. Lips just ripe to be kissed.

"*I'm* free," he volunteered. "I could—"

"Need you here, Longfellow," Bill cut him off, and the youth scowled.

"Hell, the ranch ain't going nowhere," Mitt boomed. "Come visit us when your, ahh, business with Elena is finished."

Liddy stared at the perfumed summons Bill was now folding back up. Josh saw her cheeks flush with the anger of a woman scorned.

"Yes, *Mister* Hickok," she said archly. "Do come visit once your 'business' is complete."

"Whoa there, Ignatius!" Martha "Calamity Jane" Burke shouted, tightening the reins wrapped around her hand. *"Whoa*, you ugly, humpbacked son of the Sahara."

With a raucous braying noise loud enough to wake snakes, the big, ungainly camel Jane was riding came to a jerky halt. A dozen more camels likewise halted in the pale moonlight.

"Drink up, you goldang bottomless water tanks," Jane called out as she gave the reins enough slack to let Ignatius, the herd leader, drink with the rest.

Every one of the shaggy brown camels was branded on the left hip with the "Lazy M" of the McGinnis brand. Very few peelers—experienced horse trainers like Jane—would even work with camels. They had first been imported by the U.S. Army back in '56. They proved to be great workers under very hard conditions in the desert southwest. But sadly, the very sight of them made all the other animals stampede. Besides, camels were deadly accurate spitters (as well as kickers) who fought back hard when they were whipped.

Nonetheless, the Army wanted to keep a small herd broke to saddle. A camel, some wag had joked, was just a horse designed by a committee. But Calamity Jane had come to admire them for their own qualities. In fact, the outcast Jane was close enough in spirit to truly understand this sturdy but cantankerous animal. The camel's nature was just like hers: too stubborn to submit, too tough to defeat.

The herd hadn't drunk for two days, so Jane knew they'd stay at the pond for some time. She swung down from her sheepskin-pad saddle to stretch the kinks out of her muscles. Ignatius, who was devoted to his trainer, swung his ugly, dish-flat face around to nuzzle her shoulder.

"God A'mighty, you smell like a buffalo wallow," Jane said with gruff fondness. "Or is that me?"

Jane was a stout young woman with a homely, careworn face. Her hair was tied in a heavy knot that dangled under an immaculate gray John B. Stetson hat. She wore frayed men's trousers, a beaded leather jerkin, and men's hobnailed boots. A big Smith & Wesson Volcanic pistol was tucked into a bright-red sash around her waist.

While the camels tanked up, Jane walked around the area in the moonlight, searching for a sign. Soon she found it in a nearby draw—a place where a number of riders had rested to graze their horses.

Jane also found a set of deep wagon ruts, fresh made, and she cussed out loud. "You damned thievin' barn rats!"

She knew it almost *had* to be the missing church bell. Jane was raised a Methodist of the "shouting order," and she wanted no truck with these popish Catholics. But she knew all about the famous church in Chimayo from which the bell was stolen, El Santuario. Near the altar, there was a hole in the floor filled with "miracle dirt" that supposedly healed. People claimed that, no matter how much was taken out, the hole never got larger.

But why in tarnal blazes, Jane asked the moon-lit New Mexican night, *would anyone want that bell?*

Sure, bells had been melted down before to make munitions. But only during serious war shortages did anyone bother. Well, anyhow, that missing bell had sure-God devastated the folks of Chimayo. They *believed* that old Curse of Hidalgo business. And Jane was not one to gainsay the supernatural.

The supernatural . . . in that phosphorescent moonlight, Jane turned her right palm up and gazed at a deep groove in it that ran from the heel of the palm up to the base of her index finger: her "love line," that palmist in Old El Paso had assured her. The old visionary's third eye also confirmed what a lovestruck Jane felt in her heart of hearts: Her life was meant to intertwine with Wild Bill Hickok's like two separate but intimately close strands of rope. Bill didn't realize it yet, was all.

Bill. Thinking of the handsome frontiersman caused her a pang of irony. After years of faithfully following him, a witness to his numerous intrigues with women, Jane had finally given up and gone her own way. And now look. *He* was coming to her! Destiny . . .

Jane had first heard the exciting rumor from local Pueblo Indians and their "moccasin telegraph": Wild Bill Hickok had pointed his bridle toward the Land of the Thunderbird. Soon he would arrive in the city white men called Holy Faith.

Again, just before she returned to the stock pond, Jane gazed at her love line. Call it Fate. Her love was coming to join her. But wherever Bill Hickok went, trouble followed him like a cat on a rat.

Jane stared at the wagon ruts again. The Lord had not yet enlightened Bill, had not convinced him yet that he and Jane were meant to ride the same trail through life. Until Bill finally woke up, Jane was determined to protect him.

Ignatius brayed happily when Jane returned. Deerflies were pesky near the water, and the sated animals were ready to move on. In less than a half hour, Jane drove them through the yard gate of the Lazy M and turned them out in their holding pen.

Jane forked some fodder over the rail fence, then headed toward her room in an old milking shed, stuffing a pipe with strong Mexican tobacco while she walked. From the ridges behind the low, adobe-and-stone ranch house, a coyote howled. The mournful sound sent a shiver down Calamity Jane's back.

Again Jane recalled the look of hell-spawned fear she had seen in the eyes of those who lived in Chimayo. And again she pictured those deep wagon ruts in the draw.

"Keep your nose to the wind, Wild Bill," she said softly to the night. "Hell's a-popping."

El Lobo took the whip from its socket on the dashboard and lashed at his lethargic team.

"Mas de prisa!" he shouted to them in the darkness. "Faster, you worthless nags, or I feed you to the Apaches!"

A team of four well-muscled dray horses pulled a buckboard across the open, rolling country northeast of Santa Fe. A huge church bell occupied much of the bed, tied down with ropes to prevent sudden shifting. Ten riders accompanied El Lobo Flaco, the Skinny Wolf. They were a hard-bitten lot, half of them renegade Jicarilla

Apaches, the other half former lancers who had deserted the Mexican army. Behind El Lobo's buckboard was a second, filled with forage for the horses.

Nothing was visible in the pale moonlight except saltbush cactus and yucca. El Lobo had chosen to move the bell only at night, forcing any would-be attackers to move in close. How many people knew the truth about the bell he wasn't sure. But until he got it safely to Los Cerrillos, he was taking no chances.

Many fools chased after chimeras. Like Gran Quivira, the mythical City of Gold that Coronado chased like a shadow across a fool's dream. But this bell behind him was no myth. El Lobo did not chase after phantasms.

At Caliente Springs they stopped to breathe and water the horses. El Lobo clambered into the back of the buckboard to check the ropes securing the bell. In the generous moonwash, he saw the words cast into the rim of the stolen bell: *Saint Joseph, pray for us!*

The bandit kingpin was superstitious, if not religious. That invocation of St. Joseph troubled him. Could divine intervention explain the recent arrival of this *gringo famoso*, Wild Bill Hickok?

"Well," El Lobo said out loud, "we must pass through the bitter waters before we reach the sweet."

For now Frank Tutt was keeping a close eye on Hickok. And Tutt was the best killer El Lobo had ever had on his payroll. Not only was Tutt motivated by the bounty on Hickok—his brother's blood cried out for vengeance.

Besides, there was no proof Hickok had come here to retrieve that bell. But if he had?

"Then the battle lines are clearly drawn," El Lobo said softly, ringing the bell lightly with his knuckles. "Saint Joseph and Wild Bill versus El Lobo and the devil."

Chapter Five

"Every time we meet a pretty girl," Josh fumed, "you claim dibs and keep every other fellow from trying his luck."

"That's bunk, kid. You're needed here, is all."

Wild Bill said this as he keyed the lock of his door and carefully nudged it open, making sure his hotel room was secure.

"Needed for what? To shine your boots?"

"Thanks for the offer, but the hotel does that. What we need from you is to stay in your room while I'm gone. Keep your eyes and ears open. I showed you how to hold a glass to the wall—check my room now and then for noises."

" 'While I'm gone,' " Josh repeated sarcastically from the doorway behind Bill. "That could be all night."

"If I'm lucky. I didn't come to Santa Fe for the waters. I warned you when you first bulled your way into my life, kid—I'm a one-man outfit. You swore up and down and sideways that you'd ride with me on *my* terms. Now you're trying to change horses in the middle of the stream. You ain't tethered, and this is a railhead town. You don't like the way things are, you can be back in Philly in four or five days."

"Things are okay with me," Josh sulked. "But that was just rude, Wild Bill, to practically spark with Liddy, then just toss her aside like an empty tomato can."

Bill was slapping fresh bay rum tonic on his cheeks as Josh said this. He'd put Elena's note on the oak chest-of-drawers nearby. Josh edged closer to read it.

"Rude? Kid, you know how to punctuate, but you best learn the rules of courtship, too. Liddy's a beautiful woman, and proud as a big chief. Me giving her the go-by like that, she'll take it as a challenge. Turns me into twice the prize, in her eyes."

Josh was close enough now to glance down and read the brief note:

Wild Bill, please come at once. And come alone. My home is number 17, Calle Linda. Elena Vargas.

"Besides," Bill added as he smoothed his neat mustache with one finger, admiring himself in the mirror, "I forgot all about Elena settling in Santa Fe."

"Or you'd've been there by now," Josh observed with jealous pique, still staring at the note. *Come alone.* And when Bill had his way with the beautiful Elena, there was still Liddy McGinnis out at the Lazy M. The man had himself a larder of females.

Bill ignored the remark. "Is your pistol loaded?" he asked Josh, ushering him out of the room and locking the door.

Josh nodded.

"Good. Keep it handy. And if you happen to spot that kid who runs the wash house, just ignore him. I'll talk to him later."

Bill had met the alluring Spanish beauty Elena Vargas while working his first case for Allan Pinkerton. She was proud, fiercely independent, and thanks to Bill, incalculably wealthy.

Hickok had exposed the criminal machinations of her wealthy entrepreneur fiancé. Upon his death at the hands of angry Sioux warriors, Elena inherited his business fortune. Wild Bill had sweet memories of the time he enjoyed her considerable charms. Now her terse note hinted that she, too, had similar memories—and hoped to revive them.

Despite the cloak of darkness shrouding Santa Fe, Bill remained alert and vigilant as he emerged from the hotel and strolled two blocks north to Calle Linda. It was one of the city's premier residential streets, lined with walled mansions and terraced gardens.

Number seventeen was a gray-granite villa with tall, lancet-arched windows in the style of medieval Spanish cathedrals. Bill clapped the brass knocker of a massive carved-oak door. An *indio* maid in a coif and a crisp white apron ushered him into the main salon.

"Bill! Thank God you came!"

Elena had been sitting at a beautiful rosewood piano, listlessly tapping out scales. She rose and glided across the room to offer him her hand.

The woman's abundant beauty struck Bill with physical force. Wide, sea-green eyes were set like gems behind the delicate and prominent cheekbones. Flawless mother-of-pearl skin offset raven-black hair pulled back under a silver tiara. She wore a pretty white sateen dress with black velvet trim.

"Why wouldn't I?" he countered. "Why wouldn't *any* man with blood in his veins? You never leave my mind for long, Elena."

"Nor you mine. I think often, shamelessly often," she added teasingly, "about our time together. But when I feel certain . . . desires, I defeat them by reciting the Lord's Prayer backwards. I confess, by now I recite it quite smoothly."

"Well, tonight you won't have to defeat those desires," Bill assured her. "You're here . . . I'm here. Shall we make beautiful music together?"

Bill had already kissed Elena's slim white hand. Now he moved his lips toward hers. But she eluded him with an agile little spin like a ballet twirl.

"You are a master at temptation. However, the only music we may make together, Señor Hickok, is on the piano."

Elena held up her left hand. A huge diamond sent off heliographs of light in the reflection of the gas lights.

"I am engaged," she announced.

Bill stared at the ring as if it had spit on him. His first vain reaction was an inner sting of anger. By now the likewise beautiful—and fully *available*—Liddy McGinnis had put Bill's name in her bad book. He forgot all about his glib bragging to Josh concerning "the rules of courtship." He thought, instead, about that proverbial bird in the hand—the one he had just let go.

"I'm so happy for you," Bill said sarcastically.

"He's a wonderful man, Bill," Elena said, ignoring his disappointment. "I hope you'll meet him soon. He's a captain at Fort Union. Right now he's on patrol down near Albuquerque."

Elena led him through a floored breezeway to show Bill the lush garden out back. It included a 180-foot lily pond with built-in islands. An elegant gazebo stood on one of them.

But clearly Elena had not summoned Bill so dramatically just to announce her engagement and boast about her house. They returned to the salon. A tall case clock in one corner chimed the quarter-hour, and it seemed to remind her of her real purpose.

"Come to the library, Bill. Someone is waiting to see you."

Elena took his hand again and led Bill to a paneled door. It opened onto a huge, luxuriously appointed room lined on three walls with leather-spined books in Spanish and English. Flames crackled in the Italian-marble fireplace. A walnut sideboard was crowded with bottles of liquor—including Old Taylor.

But it was the big, grinning man with the badge of a U.S. marshal pinned to his rawhide vest who got Bill's attention. The lawman had been studying a wall map of the territory when they came in. Now he hurried forward to shake the hand of his best former deputy.

"Sam! Sam Baxter!" Bill exclaimed, feeling genuine pleasure as he gave his old friend a hearty grip. "Still alive, you ornery old warhorse."

"Too mean to die, J. B. Well, I see you *have* become quite the dandy. Dressed like a barber's clerk. And you smell like a French whor—"

Sam caught himself just in time. "Pardon my range manners, Miss Vargas."

"Territorial marshal now, huh?" Bill remarked, for Sam had been assigned to Kansas when Bill rode for him.

Sam nodded his weather-grizzled head. He was a big, strong man starting to go soft with age. His hair was still full, but whiter now than Bill remembered it. And there was the start of a belly drooping over his cowhide belt. Bill could remember the day when Sam Baxter could hurl an ax forty yards and stick it into any tree—or man—you pointed out to him.

"Been out here six years now, J. B. One more and I retire on pension. Got me some stock options on a sweet little turquoise-mining operation down near the Laguna Pueblo."

"Glad to hear it." Bill glanced from Sam to Elena, suspicion cankering at him. "But I got a hunch you two didn't set up this meeting to make small talk."

"No," Sam admitted. "I got this problem."

"*We* have this problem," Elena corrected him.

"Jesus, I need a drink," Bill announced, helping himself to some bourbon.

"J. B.," Sam continued, "would you consider— just temporarily, I mean—being deputized again?"

"Not for all the king's ransom," Hickok assured him. "So save your wind."

"Oh, Bill," Elena pleaded, placing a hand on his arm. "At least hear Marshal Baxter out. I have callused my knees praying before the Santo Niño and the saints. Praying for help. Your arrival is *not* coincidental."

Bill scowled. "I'm listening, damn it."

"You ever heard," Sam asked him, "of El Lobo Flaco? The Skinny Wolf?"

"Heard the name a time or two, is all. I been pretty far north these last few years."

"He's rough, J. B. Rough as a badger out of its hole. His clan were stirring up trouble out here even before General Kearney raised the Stars and Bars over New Mexico Territory. Six years now I been tryin' to slap irons on that brown devil. But it's like trying to catch a fly with chopsticks."

"A man can't catch all the bad ones, Sam, you know that. Hell, you taught me that."

Baxter ignored him, forging on. "For years now he's terrorized the country between El Paso and Santa Fe. Robbery, rape, murder. He forces the local Indians to pay tribute—which is basically a death sentence, since most of them are dirt poor."

"Sounds like a real scrubbed angel," Bill said, adding pointedly: "I wish *you* luck in nabbing him, Sam."

"Two years ago I did manage to hind-end him with buckshot. And I had a deputy who bent a gun barrel over his head. But I found that deputy a month later with six bullets in him. And the last time I seen El Lobo, I adiosed in a hurry. There's maybe ten, a dozen riders with him these days—none of 'em schoolteachers, neither."

Bill poured himself another drink and looked at Elena. "It's obvious how this El Lobo is a headache for Sam. But what's your mix in all this?"

69

"A bell," Elena replied. "And a church. And the people of the town of Chimayo."

At the mention of Chimayo, Bill had a brief image of that terrified old Indian woman.

"The Curse of Hidalgo," he said quietly.

"Yes! *Preciso!* You know about it?"

"I've just heard of it," Bill said. "I rode through there a couple days back."

"My father," Elena explained, making the sign of the cross for his departed soul, "attended the church there for many years. He had become the *patron* of Chimayo. Now I bear this same responsibility for those who live there."

"The church there," Baxter explained, "is called El Santuario. It's special to many of the locals."

"Any church is important down here," Elena said. "But El Santuario is a sort of healing shrine. As a special mark of humility, everyone—wealthy, old, infirm—crawls up to the altar rail. Pilgrims come—used to come—from as far away as Chihuahua, Mexico. Now, however, the curse of Padre Hidalgo has been invoked on the place. Because El Lobo has stolen the bell."

"The bell?" Bill repeated, confused. "Why?"

"This bell," Elena assured him, "is different. It rings with a mellower, sweeter tone. And many swear the blind can see while that bell is ringing. That is why Padre Hidalgo invented the curse: to make sure the residents of Chimayo protect that bell."

"The curse makes them, the people, responsible for the bell," Sam told him. "Until it's returned, nothing but bad fortune and tragedy can afflict Chimayo and its residents. Even if they leave. Hell, you know me, J. B. I ain't got no more religion than a rifle has. But it *is* uncommon queer

70

how things have gone to hell in Chimayo since El Lobo and his bunch heisted that bell. Cows have dried up, seed blows out of the ground, now this plague."

"That ain't nearly so queer, Sam, as why El Lobo would take the bell in the first place," Wild Bill pointed out. "Why in hell would he *want* it?"

Sam cleared his throat.

"Miss Vargas," he spoke up, "I don't mean to be rude. But can I speak to Mr. Hickok in private now?"

"Of course, Marshal."

Just before she shut the door behind her, Elena added in a plaintive voice: "*Please*, Bill? It does not matter if you believe the curse. The people of Chimayo do. A few have already committed suicide in their fear. If that bell is not returned, more tragedy will befall them."

Sam did not immediately resume his narration after Elena left. Instead, he poured himself a neat whiskey, toasted Bill, and downed it. He gestured around the elegant room.

"Far cry from the demimonde dives of our old days, huh, J. B.?"

Bill grinned. "You remember drinking that potato whiskey in Plainview, Kansas?"

Sam slapped a stocky thigh. "Jesus hell! Remember? It took the enamel off my teeth!"

The laughter trailed off.

"All right," Bill said reluctantly. "Why did El Lobo take that damn bell?"

"Keep this close to your vest. Even Elena doesn't know it. That bell is actually seven hundred and fifty pounds of solid gold. It's got a thin coating of iron and paint to hide it."

Bill nodded. "This Hidalgo knew that. So he

makes up a curse that forces the faithful to protect the bell."

"The way you say. I knew something didn't add up about the Wolf taking a bell. So I done some checking with a professor at Santa Fe College. It was common practice back in the days of Coronado and the Spanish conquistadors. Down in South America, top-quality gold was mined by the Incas. The priests stole some of it and had it melted into bells. That way it eluded detection by their soldier escorts. Lots of them bells ended up in belfries all around this area."

Bill nodded. "Sure. And you heard Elena—the bell rings with a sweeter, mellower tone. Gold will do that. That may be how El Lobo even knew it was gold."

"Could be. I can't tell what the hell he's up to, 'zacly. I do know he's headed for Taos right now. But the Wolf ain't lettin' nobody get too close. No starmen, anyhow."

"Sam, I'll ask you the same thing I asked Elena. What's *your* mix in all this? Gold heisted from South America is out of the jurisdiction of U.S. marshals."

"Not this gold, on account it's owed to Uncle Sam. See, twelve years ago, with the U.S. Army caught up in the Civil War, the government was short on escort troops for bullion coaches. The U.S. Mint in Denver bought a shipment of gold from Mexico."

"And El Lobo," Bill supplied, "commandeered it, right?"

"Right as rain. That fortune bankrolled his operation for over a decade. Now the ruthless parasite needs more. But the U.S. government figures that bell is owed to them."

"You give it to the government," Bill pointed out, "and you haven't helped the citizens of Chimayo. Or Elena."

"Damn it, I know that. And I don't like it none. But I got a job to do, Bill. And I need your help. You're the only man I ever broke in who went on to make more arrests than I did. I'd have to deputize you, though. If it's the money—"

"It ain't, Sam. It's just . . . I came south to relax and have a good time. Besides, I'm already busy trying to save my hide from some bushwhacking son of a bitch."

"Nothing," Baxter pleaded, "could change your mind?"

"Sorry, Sam. Not for love nor money."

A lace curtain liner suddenly billowed outward in a breeze. Wild Bill started at the movement, his right hand twitching. Sam Baxter saw this and nodded. He forced out a long, fluming sigh.

"Yeah, I see how it is with you, J. B. Who's trying to kill you now?"

Bill shook his head. "Can't tell you yet. But whoever it is, he's leaving me a clue each time he tries. I got the feeling he wants me to *know* who he is before he does it. That means revenge is his main motive, not just the bounty on my hide."

"Revenge," Marshal Baxter agreed. "Which, in your case, only narrows the suspects down to about half the men in the West."

Chapter Six

Bill took the rear service entrance when he returned to La Fonda. He stopped by the front desk first, then the kid's room. Josh had broken down his LeFaucheux six-shooter and had the parts spread out before him on the escritoire, giving them a light coat of gun oil.

"Quiet night?" Bill asked.

Josh nodded. "Nothing to report. Except that Chinese kid is back on duty at the wash house. The water heater is still shut down, but now he's heating bathwater in kettles on a Sibley stove."

"I'll talk to him tomorrow. The hell you sulking about, Longfellow?"

"I'm not sulking."

"Hell you ain't. If your bottom lip was any lower, you'd be walking on it."

"It's just . . . I wanted to go back to the Lazy M with Mitt and Liddy."

"With Liddy, you mean."

"So?" Josh bristled. "Nobody can enjoy cakes and ale except Wild Bill Hickok, is that it?"

Bill didn't bother telling Josh, but a messenger from the Lazy M had left another invitation for Hickok and the kid at the front desk, urging them to visit. Bill noticed only Mitt had signed it.

"Well, Philadelphia Kid, don't get your blood in a boil and shoot me," he said. "The Lazy M is only ten miles south of town. We'll ride out there tomorrow. Maybe you can get you some 'cake.'"

Josh looked up from the trigger mechanism he was oiling, eyes narrowing in speculation as he studied Hickok. The youth laid the trigger group aside and eased the watch out of his fob pocket. He thumbed back the cover.

"Man alive! It's not even eleven P.M. and the great Lothario of the West is turning in?"

"Figure I'll play a few hands of five-card first."

"So how's Elena?" Josh asked slyly.

"Engaged," Bill answered.

"Yeah, but in what?"

"To be married, you young dolt."

"Well, what'd she want with you? It was important enough to send an urgent summons. And you deserted a winning hand."

Not to mention a comely lass, Bill thought. But out loud he said, "Kid, it don't matter two jackstraws what she wants, you take my drift? Ain't you got enough sensational stories, what with pitfall traps and exploding water heaters?"

Bill's voice rose more than he'd intended, for in fact guilt was gnawing at him. He had said no to Sam and Elena, and damn it, he *meant* it. To hell with their golden bell!

Sam had taken it like a trooper. But Bill liked

and admired Sam Baxter—the man had taught him much, early on, and those teachings were why Bill was still alive today. As for Elena . . . she had tried to buck up and accept it when Bill flat out refused to help. But her chin had crumpled in a way that sent guilt lancing through Hickok.

"Kid," Bill vowed with quiet, almost desperate determination right before he left. "We *will* paint this damned mud-color town red. We *are* going to have a good time, damn it. Whiskey, women, song, we'll drink life to the lees. I swear to God we will!"

For all his determined boasting, however, Wild Bill went to bed—all alone, yawning like an old pensioner—only one hour after his return to the hotel.

Bill propped a chair under the doorknob to reinforce the flimsy night latch. His bed was soft, and he slept the sleep of the just for most of the night. But trouble arrived in the still, quiet hours just before dawn—aptly named the "dead quiet" since most people die between two and five A.M.

Wild Bill had enjoyed pleasurable dreams all night, drifting from the arms of Liddy McGinnis to the lips of Elena Vargas. Abruptly, a shattering crash sent fragments of the room's west window exploding into the room.

Before he was even fully awake, Wild Bill rolled off the opposite side of the bed, taken over by the survival reflexes of a cat.

Even as he hurtled toward the floor, Bill tugged his gunbelt off the bedpost. By the time he hit the floor, fully awake now, he had drawn a Colt and cocked the hammer. Still not sure what was happening, he used the bed for cover while he tried to confirm a target.

Wild Bill heard the hollow drumbeat of hooves below in the street as a rider escaped. He saw the broken window and tensed, expecting dynamite to explode at any moment. But he couldn't hear a fuse sizzling—did it go out?

A fist thonked on the door.

"Wild Bill!" Josh called out. "You okay?"

"Hang on, kid."

Bill stood up, holstered his gun again, and opened the jet on a wall-mounted gaslight. He stepped into his trousers, then let Joshua in.

"What happened?" the reporter demanded. He held his pinfire revolver muzzle down.

"You got here quick, Longfellow. Good work."

Bill crossed to a burlap-wrapped rock that lay in the midst of broken shards of glass. Staying low to avoid the window, he unwrapped the cloth. Smudged on it, evidently in charcoal, was the solitary letter *D*.

"Holy—!" Josh stared at it, his eyes glinting with renewed excitement. This was becoming one hell of a mystery—and Josh's readers enjoyed the who and why far more than they cared about the what, when, and where.

"What's it mean?" Josh demanded. "First eighteen. Then sixty-five. Now the letter *D*. And two attempts to kill you."

"Those attempts weren't meant to kill me, exactly," Bill speculated out loud. "Injure me, maybe, and scare the crap out of me, sure. But mostly I think they were meant to play on my mind. To unstring my nerves."

"You know who's doing this, don't you?"

Bill gazed at the burlap and the dark letter *D*, pulling on the point of his chin.

"By now," he replied, "yeah, I think maybe I do."

77

"Who?" Josh pestered.

"You been to high school, Longfellow. You figure it out. I'm going back to bed. Tomorrow we'll talk to that Oriental kid about that water heater. Then we'll ride out to the Lazy M."

"Aw, c'mon, Bill! Who—"

"You bolted to that floor, kid? I said I'm going back to bed. Get the hell out of here before I boot you in your skinny ass."

The next morning Wild Bill and Josh were among the first patrons in the La Fonda's grand dining room. After a hearty breakfast of eggs *relleno* and spicy *chorizo* sausage, washed down with black coffee, they headed out back to the hotel wash house.

"That pitfall trap was no accident," Josh remarked. "But you know? The boiler could've been."

"Sure," Bill replied. "And pigs don't grunt, neither."

The damaged wall had already been repaired. The big, brass-trimmed water heater sat silent as a locomotive in a train shed. A Sibley stove—basically just a sheet-iron cone open at top and bottom with a pipe fit to the top to vent smoke—was being used to heat bathwater.

The place was almost deserted. They found the Chinese kid folding towels into a linen closet near the defunct heater. He paled noticeably when he saw Wild Bill Hickok advancing toward him.

"Help you, sir?" the kid said in heavily accented English, bowing deferentially.

"Hope so. That boiler explosion yesterday—it was no accident, was it?"

"*Big* accident," the kid insisted. "Machine very dangerous, yes? All time, blow up."

Bill's gunmetal eyes bored into the evasive kid. He squirmed like a bug under a pin.

"Who paid you," Bill said quietly, "to lock that pressure-release valve shut?"

"Big accident," the kid repeated. "Boilers, *whoom*! All time, blow up. Very dangerous."

"Yeah, you said that already."

Wild Bill eyed the kid. Obviously he was lying. But he was also scared. Bill felt sorry for him. The Chinese had a hard row to hoe in America, much harder than that of European immigrants. Shunned and despised, they stuck with their own and held to the values and way of life of their ancestors in Hunan Province or Canton. Without them, the transcontinental railroad could never have been built. But despite their good service to America, they were easy scapegoats when times got lean.

"It wasn't money, was it?" Bill said quietly. "Somebody threatened you, right? Said he'd kill you if you didn't diddle with that boiler?"

The kid looked nervously all around. Finally he nodded.

"Not kill me. Say kill family."

Bill nodded. "So that's the way of it. You know the man's name?"

The kid shook his head. "Never see him before."

"Know where's he's staying?"

Again a shake of the head.

"White man?"

The kid nodded. "Young man. Maybe little older than him."

The kid pointed at Joshua. "Mean man. Handsome face, but hard eyes like stones, crooked mouth."

"All right, son." Wild Bill patted the kid's skinny shoulder. He slipped him a silver dollar. " 'Preciate it."

"No tell on me?" the kid pleaded.

"No tell. I promise."

"So who is it?" Josh pressed Wild Bill as the two men took the service stairs back up to the second floor. "Still think you know?"

Bill ignored him, alone with his own thoughts.

"Will there be more attacks?" Josh demanded.

"You can put it down in your book. Somebody means to free my soul."

"Well, if I can put *that* down," Josh complained, "why not his name, too? Why do you always make a fellow beg like a starving Indian?"

"There, there, that's a tough old soldier," Bill mocked as Josh unlocked his door. "You damned Philadelphia bawl-baby. Throw together some duds, kid. We're riding out to the Lazy M to see Mitt and Liddy."

The morning air was still and hot, the windmills motionless as paintings. Wild Bill and Josh followed the Old Pecos Trail southeast out of Santa Fe. Although it was a short ride to the Lazy M, it was mostly an ascending trail. They held their mounts to a trot, walking them now and then to spell them.

Mountain ranges flanked them in the distance, sliced by gullies on their lower slopes. They passed a few big spreads with cattle, but mostly just little half-section nester farms. Sometimes the dwellings, on these smaller homesteads, were little more than brush shanties covered with wagon canvas. An intricate system of *acequias* irrigated the corn, beans, and squash, all controlled by a mother ditch with huge gates.

Wild Bill kept a vigilant eye on all the good ambush points. But he found time, now and then, to cast a humorous glance toward Josh. The kid, showing his streak of gumption, had insisted on riding Old Smoke, his nemesis. Now Josh sat rigid in the saddle, grim-faced and determined, looking to get bucked at any moment. But by God, he *would* tame that horse!

"Aw, c'mon, Bill," Josh resumed his pestering at one point. "Who was it tossed that rock through your window last night?"

Bill's eyes cut to the rimrock above them. He recalled the Chinese kid's words: *Mean man. Handsome face, but hard eyes like stones.*

"That's a stumper, ain't it?" Bill replied.

Josh started to protest. But Old Smoke edged close to a cactus-covered hummock, and the kid prepared to protect his still-aching sitter. Wild Bill snorted, waiting for the wily gray to "chin the moon" and send the kid flying.

They passed the occasional Pueblo *indio* walking on the trail. The wealthiest ones proudly displayed their turquoise-and-silver jewelry. In a land where Indians were still forbidden, by edict, from riding horses, turquoise had become their leading sign of status. Indeed, its distinctive color—known as Taos Blue—was seen everywhere.

Some of the Pueblos gave them shy, friendly greetings. Others, however, gazed with mute fear at the Winchester rifle protruding from Bill's saddle boot—"the sticks which speak like the Thunder Bird." Bill knew some of them were recalling the glorious Pueblo Revolt of 1680, one of the few times when local Indians overcame intertribal wars and dealt misery to the pale bearded ones.

"The numbers eighteen and sixty-five," Josh repeated, musing out loud, "and the letter *D*. What's it mean, Bill?"

Bill's eyes, narrowed to slits in the burning sun, studied the trail on both sides. For absolutely no logical reason at all, he had a sudden thought: Did the kid's question just now have anything to do with Sam, Elena, and their quest for the stolen bell?

"Nah—I'm just shooting at rovers," Bill muttered.

"What'd you say?" Josh demanded.

Again Bill's eyes cut to the rimrock above. "Never mind," he told the kid. "Shut up now and keep your eyes peeled."

Frank Tutt had been watching, from a window of his room at the Dorsey, when Hickok and the gangly pup with him had walked to the livery barn. Seeing them ride south out of town, he knew there was only one route they could take for many miles—the Old Pecos Trail.

No white man knew the Santa Fe country as well as Frank Tutt did. Working for El Lobo had taught Frank every game trace, hidden *arroyo*, or secret Indian footpath between Taos to the north and the Manzano Mountains to the south.

Thus, it was child's play to circumvent the Old Pecos Trail, by way of a more direct trace, and get out ahead of Hickok. Now Frank's sturdy little *grullo*—a dark blue gelding—was hobbled behind him in the jagged rimrock above the main trail.

Frank knew that high-heel boots, good for

holding stirrups, were not made for climbing across talus slopes and piles of loose volcanic scree. He was wearing triple-soled fawnskin moccasins, flexible but thick enough to protect the feet.

He crouched and laid his Spencer .56 carbine across a rock, screwing the 7x scope into its bracket atop the barrel-and-receiver group. Then he thumbed copper-jacketed slugs one by one through a trap in the butt plate.

By now Frank figured he'd given Hickok enough clues. The man *must* know by now who was after him. That's what Frank wanted— wanted like hell thirst—for Hickok to *know* that Dave Tutt's kid brother was avenging his death. Otherwise, there was no xreal justice to the killing of Hickok.

Down below, two riders emerged from a dogleg bend in the trail. Hickok was in the lead on a handsome chestnut with a roached mane. The kid rode perhaps ten yards behind on his gray.

Tutt's lips eased away from his teeth. He lowered his right cheek tight against the carbine's stock, sighting in on the trail below.

"Touch you for luck, Wild Bill?" he said out loud, heart palpitating with excitement now that *the* moment had finally arrived.

Frank moved the crosshairs until they were centered on Hickok's chest. He took a long breath, relaxed, slowly expelled the breath. Then his trigger finger began taking up the slack.

"Can't be far to the Lazy M now," Bill remarked when they pulled in, atop a long rise, to let the horses blow. "We're coming back down into the river valley, prime cattle grazing."

Josh breathed in deeply the clean, nose-tickling tang of green alfalfa fields. The Pecos River valley lay spread out below them, a lush green ribbon meandering through the parched brown hills surrounding it.

Rocky bluffs rose on both sides of the trail. Wild Bill studied them while they rested.

"Liddy might not be so eager to see you," Josh needled. "Way you just dumped her and went running to Elena."

"Smoke 'em if you got 'em," Bill replied, still scrutinizing the bluffs. "My loss is your gain, huh? Maybe you'll have to recite some poems to her while the doves coo?"

The horses stood snorting and stomping at flies. Bill leaned forward, resting his forearms on the saddle horn while he concentrated his attention on one point above them in the rimrock.

"See something?" Josh demanded.

Bill waved him quiet. He thought he had just seen a glitter of reflection. But there was no quartz or mica, up in that spot, to reflect sunlight—just dark shale and red sandstone.

There! Another winking glitter.

"Cover down!" Wild Bill barked.

He didn't wait for Josh to follow orders. Bill swatted the kid right out of his saddle with a mighty backhand swing that caught Josh in the chest.

Bill followed suit, jerking his feet from the stirrups and literally rolling off the rump of his horse. But even as he cleared the saddle, a rifle cracked loudly from overhead, and Josh's heart almost skidded to a stop.

Chapter Seven

Wild Bill had many years of experience when it came to being shot at. And he had figured out at least one thing for sure: Usually, you won't hear the shot that kills you. The bullet arrives before the noise of the gun.

So he was actually relieved to hear that rifle crack go echoing across the terrain. Both ambushed riders scuttled into the salt-cedar thickets beside the trail. Their horses ran a few hundred yards on down the trail, then stopped to cut grass beside a little seep spring.

Bill expected more bullets to hail in from the rimrock. Instead, a minute of silence followed that single shot.

"The sniper leave?" Josh spoke up from his hiding spot.

"How long ago was once-upon-a-time?" Bill

shot back sarcastically. "How the hell would I know?"

Moments later, more shots rang out. Bill's brows met in a puzzled frown.

"Those were pistol shots," he told Josh. "And they weren't fired at us. That was behind the ridge. Let's clear out, Longfellow."

Sticking to whatever cover they could find, the two men moved quickly ahead and caught up to their horses.

"Going back after him?" Josh demanded.

Bill, his face in shadow under his broad black hat, cast a long glance back toward the rimrock. His memories of Civil War disasters made him reluctant to attack the high ground.

"We'll leave it alone, for now. No need to go looking for our own graves. He'll leave his calling card again."

"It's the same man that threw the rock last night," Josh said, not making it a question. "The mystery man who dug that pitfall and made the Chinese kid sabotage the water boiler. 'Cept he *ain't* a mystery, is he? Not to you."

"Leave it alone," Bill repeated as he stepped up into leather. "Let's break dust."

U.S. Marshal Sam Baxter was over a barrel.

Less than a year now, and he'd be retiring from frontier law enforcement. Like a man with one last promise to fulfill, he wanted, more than he ever wanted anything, to lock away the worst public menace in the Southwest: El Lobo Flaco, the Skinny Wolf. And that gold bell the Wolf took from the people of Chimayo—it would at least partially compensate the U.S. Mint for gold he robbed.

Sam was willing, all right, but sadly unable.

Once, he had three deputies to assist him in this vast territory. But one had been gunned down in Lincoln County, and another died of snakebite down near Isleta Pueblo. His only remaining deputy stayed busy serving warrants and tracking fugitives. Without help from Cavalry or Hickok, Sam knew he didn't stand a snowball's chance of even getting close to the well-protected El Lobo.

Now, as Marshal Baxter scouted the hill country south of Santa Fe, he wished all over again that J. B. Hickok was still his deputy. Hell, with Wild Bill on his side, a man could hog-tie Geronimo himself. But Hickok had got too famous for his own good. He—

Sam's thoughts scattered like startled birds when he spotted motion from the corner of his right eye.

Sam looked up toward a sandstone ridge to his right. Thank God his old eyes were better than his kidneys—Sam spotted a rider on a sturdy *grullo*, picking its way up toward the rimrock. Sam recognized that dark blue gelding instantly: Frank Tutt's horse.

Sam had no idea exactly what Tutt was up to. The Old Pecos Trail lay on the far side of that ridge—chances were good Tutt was preparing to ambush someone. But the important thing was the fact that Tutt worked for El Lobo. If Sam could arrest him for something, maybe he could arrange a little trade: Frank's freedom in exchange for information about El Lobo's plans for the bell.

It was a long shot. But Sam had to take help where he could find it.

"C'mon, old soldier," he called to his big blood bay, shortening the reins to head him up the slope behind Tutt.

If he was a younger man, Sam would have hobbled his mount and climbed that ridge on foot. But his joints were too stove up with arthritis—he'd have to risk being spotted.

Frank disappeared over the top of the ridge. Before long Sam heard it: the clip-clop of shod hooves approaching along the trail below.

Tutt's carbine spoke its piece, the noise echoing off the surrounding ridges. Sam tossed caution to the wind and spurred his bay up the slope, drawing his short iron.

That reckless burst of speed was his fatal mistake; soon, one of his mount's hooves dislodged a good-size rock. It went clattering and clashing down the sandstone slope, causing a small but loud rock slide.

Tutt appeared into view above him, staring downward to locate the source of the racket. As Sam watched, the gunsel surprised him by setting aside his carbine at sight of the marshal.

Huh, Sam thought. Maybe he ain't the hardcase I thought he was.

But that was only to free his hands. Frank smacked the butt of his Colt Navy revolver; it swiveled up in its special-rigged holster, and fire leaped out of the muzzle.

Tutt fired three times. One slug hammered Sam's right shoulder and turned him sideways in the saddle. A second raked his rib cage, and the third almost knocked him from his horse when it punched into the side of his neck, severing the big carotid artery. An obscene gout of blood spattered the fender of his saddle.

With his last reserves of strength and consciousness, Sam rolled his bandanna and tied off the neck wound. He wheeled his mount and fled down the slope. But already awareness was ebbing. Desperately, Sam pulled a strong rawhide thong from his saddle pocket and began lashing his belt to his saddle.

There'd been other bad scrapes in his long career. But Sam knew this was probably the worst—he'd likely seen his last sunrise. The only slim chance he had was to stay on horseback and let the bay carry him to help.

After the near-fatal ambush, only twenty minutes of uneventful riding brought Wild Bill and Joshua to a pair of stately stone gateposts. They marked the turnoff from the Old Pecos Trail to the Lazy M spread.

"Judging from the size of that bunkhouse," Bill remarked, nodding at the sprawling, cottonwood-log structure, "Mitt's got at least a dozen riders. I'd guess that means his herd's at least thirty thousand strong. Prob'ly up higher in the summer pastures now."

Mitt McGinnis was perched on the top rail of the breaking pen, watching a Mexican peeler being bucked half to death by an unbroken coyote dun. His sister Liddy stood behind Mitt. She watched in fascinated horror at the peeler's apparent indifference to his own health. She wore a crisp white blouse tucked into a blue riding skirt. The long blond hair was pulled into a knot on her neck.

Mitt spotted the new arrivals and waved his hat at them. He leaped down athletically to greet them.

"Wild Bill! Joshua! This makes my day, boys! Welcome, welcome. Manuel!" he added in a shout, and the *mozo* came running from the nearby stables. "Take care of their horses, son. C'mon up to the house, gents, and wash the trail off your faces."

Liddy, in contrast to her brother, was much cooler in manner as her blue, wing-shaped eyes appraised Wild Bill. "Free to visit us so soon? And how was Miss Vargas? Well, I trust?"

"Yes. And happily engaged to a soldier at Fort Union."

"Oh? You must have been . . . taken aback by that news?"

"Liddy," Bill said with his most winning smile, "I believe your claws are showing."

"That's 'Miss McGinnis,'" she corrected him with icy hauteur.

Deliberately snubbing Wild Bill, Liddy turned to Josh. She walked closer to the surprised youth, moving with catlike grace. She gave him a low-lidded smile that made his heart race.

"So. Mr. Robinson. How are you?"

"Please call me Josh."

"Only if you'll call me Liddy," she insisted, making sure Bill heard her. "My lands, Josh! I saw your byline on a story in *The New Mexican*. It must be wonderful, having such influence on contemporary society."

Josh swelled up with pride, and Bill had to snort. The kid was so green, he couldn't recognize it when he was being wrapped around a wily lady's finger.

"Add all his 'influence' to a nail," Bill chipped in, "and you'll have a nail."

Liddy turned on him like an attack dog. "You're just envious—and no doubt feeling guilty," she accused Bill. "Josh is so young, yet he's doing something *so* constructive with his life."

"Lad's a saint," Bill agreed from a deadpan. He scratched a phosphor to life with his thumbnail and lit a cheroot.

"Come along, Josh," Liddy said to the over-whelmed youth. "There's just enough time before dinner. We'll saddle you a fresh horse, and I'll show you my brother's ranch. Just the two of us," she added for Bill's benefit.

"She's a mite miffed at you, Bill," Mitt apologized when Liddy and Josh were out of earshot. "You ruffled her female feathers by going to see Elena."

"Women," Bill replied with a shrug as the two men walked toward the house. "I can read tracks on bare rock. But I'm damned if I can read the female heart."

Despite his dismissive manner, Bill was in a foul mood, all right. The whole point of this trip south was to cut loose the wolf a bit. So far, though, he'd spent most of his time dodging attempts on his life. And he wasn't even getting paid for it.

Mitt, who was still a bachelor at thirty, showed off his fine, ten-room house while the two old friends cut the dust with some excellent Irish sipping whiskey. They settled into comfortable wing chairs in Mitt's library, a huge room lined with leather-bound classics.

"You've come a long way from your soddy in Kansas," Bill complimented his friend.

Mitt shrugged modestly, though the words clearly pleased him.

"Ahh—you know how it is, Bill. He who rolls up his sleeves seldom loses his shirt. I wouldn't have a pot to spit in if it hadn't been for you. A good starman is a national treasure."

Outside, there was a raucous braying noise that made Bill wince and Mitt grin.

"God kiss me," Bill remarked. "One of your hands skinning mules alive?"

"You just heard one of the camels, Billy. This camel operation of mine is just chicken fixin's, far as the money. Mainly I'm doing it as a favor to the Army out here. But as far as the *entertainment*, it's priceless. I swear I don't know who's more of a caution—them camels or that ripe-smelling she-devil I hired to break them."

A cloud of suspicion suddenly darkened Wild Bill's face.

"Ripe-smelling she-devil?" he repeated, his tone flat with sudden apprehension. "What she-devil might that be, Mitt?"

Mitt never answered. For at that moment a Mexican maid in a lace apron and starched mob-cap poked her head into the library.

"Dinner will be served in thirty minutes, *señors*. Carlita has prepared rooms for both of our guests. Shall I show you to your room, Señor Wild-Bill?"

Both men grinned. Obviously the young girl thought "Wild Bill" was one word, and this man's last name. Bill followed her to a roomy, sunny bedroom in the west wing of the sprawling house. A water basin, towels, and shaving accessories had been laid out for him. Bill washed, shaved, and changed into his best black suit.

While he spruced up, Bill again ran the clues through his mind: the numbers 18 and 65, the letter *D*. There was also the Chinese kid's claim that the man who threatened him was about Josh's age.

"Bet you a dollar to a doughnut hole," Bill told his reflection in the cheval glass mirror, "it's

Frank Tutt. All jacked up on those Rebel lies about how I plugged his brother Dave in the back."

But why couldn't Bill shake the suspicion that this vendetta to kill him was also connected, somehow, to the stolen church bell?

The four of them ate dinner at an English gateleg table with a fancy ivory lace tablecloth, set with fine, bone-white china. Liddy looked radiant in a low-cut gown of silver satin, her opalescent skin flawless as moonstone.

She insisted that Josh sit beside her and made a point of fussing over him during the meal. Liddy acted as if Bill weren't even present in the room. But Mitt and Bill, like any good friends on the frontier, had plenty of reminiscing and catching up to do.

"I envy you, Bill," Mitt declared between the bisque and the main course, baby rack of lamb. "You came out here to New Mex as a boy Josh's age. That means you got here in time for the last of the old Taos Fairs. Mixed in with Ceran St. Vrain, Kit Carson, Charles Bent, and that crowd. No lawyers and no taxes in those days. Men settled their own scores."

"That's *barbaric*," Liddy protested, joining their conversation for the first time. "You can't have civilized society without rules."

"Oh, there were rules," Bill said in his amiable way. "F'rinstance, if you found a body with a bullet hole in the front, it was ruled death my misadventure. Case closed. Bullet holes in the back, however, were ruled murder."

"In other words," Liddy said sarcastically, "murder from the front was accepted. Some 'code,' Mr. Hickok. The landscape out here may be rough and majestic; the men, however, are just *rough*."

A delicious dessert of French custard ice cream was followed by after-dinner cordials. Now and then Liddy cooled herself with a palmetto fan.

"So, Mr. Hickok," Liddy said, baiting him with her tone as she smiled behind her fan. "Why don't you regale all of us with tales of your ... conquests out west? I've read that you sometimes disappear, for days at a time, in the company of some beautiful woman or other?"

Bill bowed slightly in her direction. "Well, Miss McGinnis, they say you can't tell if the wood is good just by looking at the paint."

Liddy flushed deeply, for his innuendo applied to her, also.

Liddy had gotten herself into this mess. But Josh gallantly rescued her by quickly changing the subject to the village of Chimayo. He briefly described the desperate situation there when he and Bill rode through three days ago.

Liddy lamented that the church there, El Santuario, was closed and the village quarantined.

"It is an unpretentious little chapel," she told Josh while Bill and Mitt listened. "But some insist it is the Lourdes of New Mexico. Do you know, Joshua? One entire wall is covered with the crutches of those who were healed there."

Josh gazed into her bottomless blue eyes, mesmerized. "That *is* remarkable," he said enthusiastically. "I'd love to see it with you sometime."

Bill had his belly full of this haughty bitch and her lovestruck puppy. He wiped some crumbs from his mustache with the corner of a linen napkin.

"Hunh," he said, winking at Mitt. "Think about that. All those crutches, but not one wooden leg."

Mitt, who like Wild Bill was not known for piety, burst out laughing. He got so carried away that he even smacked the table repeatedly with his fist.

Josh tried to keep a straight face, out of loyalty to Liddy. But Bill's joke *was* a capital hit. Despite his best effort, Josh, too, burst into paroxysms of mirth.

"That one's going into my next dispatch," he declared.

All this cynicism was too much for Liddy. She flushed red to her very earlobes and rose from the table, throwing down her napkin.

"All three of you are coarse and vulgar!" she accused them. "Benighted savages! It is *not* a joke what happens in Chimayo. It's terrible, simply horrid. If you were even half the man you pretend to be, Mr. Hickok, you'd help those poor people!"

"Liddy!" Josh said, rising to stop her. "Wait, I didn't mean—"

But she had already stormed out of the room in high dudgeon. Before anyone could say anything else, there was a thunder of hooves and a hideous racket of braying camels out in the yard.

"Martha's back with the herd," Mitt said. "C'mon, boys, you've got to see this. It's a caution to screech owls."

Wild Bill's dinner almost came back up at the mention of the name Martha. *Can't be*, he told himself as he and Josh followed Mitt out into the yard. What are the chances?

Dust hazed the main yard, stirred up by the camel herd. Bill spotted a familiar gray Stetson, and he groaned out loud. He was about to turn and flee back into the house. But he was too late.

"Yoo-hoo! Wild Bill! I *knew* fate would toss us together again, you purty critter!"

Martha "Calamity Jane" Burke spoke from her sheepskin-pad perch high atop the hump of the lead camel, Ignatius.

"Jane," Bill greeted her in a neutral voice while Josh covered a grin with his hand. "This is a . . . genuine surprise. Mitt didn't tell me you were working for him."

"You two know each other?" Mitt demanded. He had heard some wild tales about a woman called Calamity Jane. But this woman hadn't used that name when he hired her on.

"Not in the biblical sense," Jane retorted. "Not yet. But we will—we got us a shared destiny."

By now Liddy had been drawn out onto the porch, lured by all the commotion. She heard this last remark and saw the deep discomfort in Bill's face.

"Why, this must be serendipity!" she exclaimed with false enthusiasm. "I mean, Wild Bill and Jane meeting like this. Joshua, why don't we take a ride? That way, these two lovebirds can get reacquainted while I finish showing you the ranch."

Bill turned white as a fish belly. He turned to say something. But a camel in a foul mood chose that moment to crane its neck and spit right in Bill's face.

"Careful, handsome," Jane warned. "They're mighty jealous of my affections. And being ugly as sin, they won't abide a pretty face."

Josh and Liddy shared a laugh while a scowling Wild Bill wiped his face dry with his handkerchief.

"Rider coming in," Mitt remarked. "He's sure sittin' his saddle funny. Maybe he's hurt."

Everyone turned to watch a big, seventeen-hand blood bay trotting through the yard gate.

"Why, that's Sam Baxter," Bill said, stepping off the porch.

"So it is," Mitt agreed. "Is he sleeping? Look how his head's slumping."

Sam's horse stopped cold where it was, afraid to approach the herd of camels.

"Who's Sam Baxter?" Josh asked, but Bill ignored him. He walked out to meet his friend.

"Sam, you ugly son of trouble," Bill called to his former mentor. "Light down and . . . *Christ!*"

With an unceremonious *flump*, Sam's big body slid lopsided from the saddle and landed on the ground.

Liddy screamed, biting her knuckles. Bill rushed forward to check on the marshal.

"Dead," he announced grimly. "He took three slugs. The one in his neck severed an artery. He bled to death."

Gingerly, Bill touched some of the blood. Tacky, but not yet completely dried out. Josh came up beside him.

"He was a U.S. marshal," the reporter said, spotting Sam's five-point star.

"Best there was," Bill said tersely. "He taught me tricks that've saved my life more than once. Matter fact, kid, I think he saved *your* life, too."

"Mine? Man alive! But how? When?"

"Today. That ambush we got caught in earlier."

"Sure, I take your meaning. Those shots we heard on the other side of the ridge."

Bill nodded, still looking at Sam's seamed, lifeless face. He gave his all for America. Served and protected and never asked for a thing in return but a modest wage and the right to respect himself. Bill recalled Mitt's comment: *A good starman is a national treasure.*

"He died taking that sniper's bead off of us," Bill said thoughtfully.

Mitt came closer. "I knew Marshal Baxter as a damn good lawman. I'll have a couple hands dig him a grave. And I'll send Manuel to fetch Padre Salazar. We'll give him a decent burial."

"Send for the priest," Bill agreed. "But give *me* the shovel. It'll be an honor to dig this man's grave."

"Who did this, Bill?" Josh asked in a hushed voice.

"I got an idea, but I can't say right now. But I know Sam deserved better than this. I guess our little pleasure trip is officially over, Longfellow. Because I sure-God intend to find the bastard."

Chapter Eight

One day after he killed Marshal Baxter, Frank Tutt met with his boss in a mountain pass just northeast of San Juan Pueblo in northern New Mexico. San Juan was situated about halfway between Santa Fe to the south, and Taos to the northeast.

El Lobo and his hard-bitten riders had made camp in the lee of a long spur of rock. The crosswinds were fierce here, and colder than the lower elevations. They buffeted the men from every direction. The Apaches, as was their custom, had slept behind low windbreaks made of stones. The Mexican riders had simply wrapped themselves in their Saltillo blankets and crowded under the buckboard that carried the huge church bell.

Tutt arrived just after sunup, tired and trail-worn. He had ridden day and night to reach this rendezvous point, and he was red-eyed and snappish from exhaustion. Nor was El Lobo's mood any better. Within minutes, the two were at loggerheads.

"All right, damn it," Tutt said. "So Hickok got away this time. I killed Baxter, didn't I? He's been dogging you like a shadow for years."

"So what? Has your brain come unhinged? Killing Baxter won't earn you jewels in paradise. It is *Hickok* we must fear above all others."

For a long moment both speakers fell silent. The only sound was the horses champing grass and the wind blasting through a nearby canyon, shrieking in the caves and crevices.

"I have modified the plan," El Lobo finally resumed in his quiet, dangerous voice. "I sent Jemez"—this was the best scout among the Apaches—"to scout the country around Taos. We are in luck, 'mano. Do you remember the silver mine that used to operate there?"

Tutt nodded. In that early light, his eyes looked as hard and cold as two chips of obsidian.

"German bunch, right? Made good money until it went bust right after the war?"

El Lobo nodded. Several days' beard growth shadowed his cheeks and jaw. Silver conchos circled the brim of his low shako hat.

"The Germans are long gone, the mine sealed. But there is still forty miles of narrow-gauge railroad between the old mine and the town of Springer, which was once their freight station for the silver ore."

"So what?" Frank pried open a can of peaches with his bowie knife. He began slurping them down without a spoon. El Lobo stared in disgust at the juice dribbling off Tutt's chin.

"Our old friend Witter Boyd took over the line

and the train when the Germans pulled stakes. Now Witter runs a short-line railroad between Taos and Springer. He himself operates the steam locomotive."

"I take your drift, Wolf. That means we can shake off any followers in Taos. The trail will disappear once that bell is loaded on a train and hauled to Springer."

"Not disappear," El Lobo corrected him. "I will send a false trail north toward Colorado. We will load one buckboard in Taos and send the other one on, loaded with rocks. For a price, Witter will gladly haul the bell secretly after dark. No one will know. Then it will be a straight shot south from Springer to the smelter at Los Cerrillos. In less than one week, I will have new gold bars."

"Don't you mean *we* will have new gold bars?"

El Lobo's thin lips eased away from his teeth. In that moment he *did* resemble a wolf.

"*Chinga tu madre,*" he swore without heat. "That gold is mine. But each man who helps me will get a fair share."

By now the rest of the men were stirring to life and starting cooking fires in little pits. The Apaches and the Mexican deserters carefully avoided each other, sticking to their own groups.

"As for you," El Lobo told Frank, "I want you back on Hickok. Until you kill him, or he kills you, he must be constantly watched."

Joshua was shocked.

In the year he had personally known and observed Wild Bill Hickok, he had seldom seen the famous gunman perform any manual labor. Hickok would face down any killer in a gunfight, and he had the endurance of a doorknob. But he avoided hard work the way horses avoided bears.

Yet Wild Bill refused to let anyone else help him dig Sam Baxter's grave. Josh was further shocked when the irreverent Hickok bowed his head as the priest prayed over the departed. Almost everyone on the Lazy M, from Mitt to the lowest-paid hands, turned out in their Sunday best for the lawman's funeral.

"America was made possible by men like Sam Baxter," Bill said in a brief, quiet-spoken, but sincere eulogy. "He always gave more than he asked for, and he never gave any man an order that he wouldn't gladly carry out himself. When food was scarce, Sam was the last in line to eat. But when trouble came, he was the first man into the breach. He never got rich nor famous, but he's an American hero. No man's ghost will ever say, 'If only Sam Baxter had been a braver man.'"

Josh, like everyone else present, was deeply moved. Liddy sobbed openly, and several grizzled cowhands had to swipe a tear or two from their eyes. As the ropes holding Sam's pine coffin were lowered into the grave, Josh decided that U.S. Marshal Sam Baxter's obituary would be his next story for the *New York Herald*.

Bill Hickok was not a troubled, brooding man who wallowed in regrets. Yet Josh could tell that something was rankling at him. Even the considerable charms of Liddy McGinnis failed to interest Bill right now. Once Sam was in the ground, Bill took a bottle to his room and proceeded to get snockered.

"C'mon in, kid," Bill said when Josh appeared at his door to see how his friend was doing. "Joshua, you've always kept your word to me. If I tell you something *off the record*, does it stay that way?"

"You kidding? Is Paris a city?"

Bill nodded. Though he'd consumed half a bottle of bourbon, his speech was clear and coherent. Succinctly, he explained the real reason why Elena Vargas had sent for him on their first night in Santa Fe. Josh's eyes widened when he learned about the golden bell stolen from Chimayo.

"Sam was there waiting at Elena's house. He asked me to help him get the bell back," Bill said morosely. "But I was too busy with visions of naked flesh and straight flushes."

"You think it was this El Lobo who killed him?" Josh asked.

Bill shook his head. "No, not by his own hand. But I got a hunch now there's some kind of connection to him and that bell. The killer, I'd wager a year's pay, is a young gun tough named Frank Tutt."

"Tutt," Josh repeated. "Tutt . . . I know that name! You killed a fellow named Dave Tutt right near the end of the war."

Bill nodded. "Man was a traitor. I used to scout and spy with him for the Union. But Dave sold out for gold—told Johnny Reb all about our troop movements. Got my unit damn near massacred near Vicksburg. I ran into Dave in Springfield, Missouri, in—"

"In 1865," Josh took over the story, his voice tight with excitement, "you faced him down right in the town square, even let him make the first play. Then you planted two slugs dead to the heart."

Josh smacked his right fist into his left palm as it all came clear.

"And that's it! That explains those clues. The

numbers eighteen and sixty-five, plus the letter *D* for Dave."

Bill nodded. "I killed Dave Tutt in a fair fight. A dozen people confirmed that. But scuttlebutt went all over, how I plugged him in the back. Now Frank is determined to settle a blood score."

"So what now?" Josh asked.

Bill started to pour more liquor into a pony glass. Instead, he corked the bottle and pushed it away.

"Bring me paper, ink, and a nib," he instructed the reporter, a new resolve in his tone. "And tell Mitt I need somebody to run a message into Santa Fe."

When Josh returned to Bill's room, he watched Wild Bill pen a cryptic, one-line note: *Elena, Sam's dead and I'm on the case. Wild Bill.*

"There goes your pleasure trip," Josh remarked.

"Know what? It was gone when I rode over that pitfall trap. And now you got your next big story. Happy, scoop?"

"I s'pose," Josh said without much enthusiasm.

Bill snorted. "Christ, you look like somebody just kicked your dog. I'm wise to your disguise, kid. You don't want to leave Liddy, do you?"

Josh flushed, but he nodded. "No, not now. She's really starting to take a shine to me, Bill."

Bill had to snort again. "Longfellow, you know how to put one word after another, all right. Damn good newspaperman. And when trouble hits, you've got enough guts to fill a smokehouse. But you're still a babe in the woods when it comes to wily women."

"Wha'd'you mean?" Josh demanded, offended.

"What, did I speak Navajo? I mean Liddy, you young jackass. That little cottontail is playing you like a fiddle. She's trying to use you to make me jealous."

"That's a lie!" Josh fumed.

Bill dismissed the discussion with an impatient wave. His gunbelt hung from one of the bedposts. Hickok slid both custom-made Peacemakers from their holsters. He began breaking them down to clean and oil them.

"Leave it alone," Bill said. "Get your gear ready. We've got to move quick. It's going to be a while before you sleep in a soft bed again."

"Where we headed?"

"North to Taos. That's the direction Sam said El Lobo was headed with that bell. Since it's on the way, we're also going to stop in Santa Fe and Chimayo."

Bill stood up and moved to the window, parting the curtains. Josh watched him peer out cautiously.

"Who you looking for?" the youth demanded.

"Who else? That damned horny man-eater Calamity Jane. Hell, I'll be safer looking for killers. Hurry up and get ready. We best put this place behind us before she gets liquored up."

Only a few hours after Sam Baxter's funeral, Wild Bill and Josh were ready for the trail.

Mitt and Liddy prevailed upon their guests to stay. But that fresh grave, on a low hill behind the house, was like a prod to Bill's determination.

There was a final, brief delay while one of Mitt's wranglers pulled and reset those loose horseshoes on the sorrel. And now, Josh noticed with a bitter sting of disappointment, there had been a sea change in Liddy's attitude toward him—and toward Wild Bill.

Her haughty, flippant, prideful manner ceased. She had been badly shaken by what happened to Marshal Baxter—and by Hickok's deep-felt response. She understood now that he was heading into grave danger. It was a reminder that he hadn't gotten famous simply for intriguing with women.

Liddy contrived to catch Bill alone for a moment while he was rigging his chestnut gelding in the paddock behind the barn. But she made the mistake of coming up silently behind him. Her foot snapped a small stick. At the sound, Hickok tucked and rolled, coming up on his haunches with a .44 leveled on her.

Liddy paled, the roses in her cheeks disappearing.

"Jesus, girl," Bill admonished her as he holstered his short iron. "It's not a good idea to sneak up on a fellow like that."

"I'm sorry." Liddy swallowed the lump of fear in her throat. "Bill?"

"Hmm?" He had returned to his task.

"May I give you something for luck?"

Hickok, busy inspecting the saddle blanket for burrs, turned to look at her again.

"They say I have plenty of luck already. But you can't ever have too much. I'd be honored."

Liddy handed him a silver locket. Bill opened it. Inside, a little strand of blond hair was tied with a blue ribbon.

Liddy blushed. "It's not presumptuous of me, is it?"

"I *like* it when ladies presume," Bill assured her. He tucked the locket into the fob pocket of his vest.

Liddy moved in a little closer. Bill could smell her lilac perfume. "You'll be careful?"

" 'Careful' is my middle name."

"Will you . . . I mean, do you think you'll be riding back this way?"

Bill grinned. "Why, sure," he teased her. "I ain't had a chance to jaw with Mitt yet."

"Oh, pouf! Is that the *only* reason?"

By now Liddy's pretty face was only inches from Bill's.

"Well," he reminded her, "I'm pretty 'coarse and vulgar,' remember? Not even *half* the man I pretend to be, I think you said?"

This time Liddy flushed to the roots of her long hair.

"I spoke in the heat of anger."

"Then let's kiss and make up," Bill suggested, wrapping his arms around her.

But even before their lips met, the ground began to tremble under their feet. Bill glanced up, then went wide-eyed. A long, low stable behind the bunkhouse was used to house the camel herd. Now the ugly, ungainly desert denizens were racing toward the paddock—with Calamity Jane riding the master camel.

"Hep!" she bellowed, flailing Ignatius with a light sisal whip. "Hep! Hep!"

One sight of those strange, monstrous beasts, and Bill's horse reared up on its hind legs, whickering in panic. Bill cursed as he fought to grab the bridle—Jane had been watching him and Liddy all along!

"I'll have to take a rain check on that kiss," Bill

said in haste. He realized the chestnut was about to bolt wildly. Not wanting to waste time chasing it down, Bill leaped onto the animal. He held on for dear life as it broke for the open gate of the paddock, Liddy gaping in pure astonishment behind him.

Chapter Nine

"*Why* do we need to return to Santa Fe?" Josh complained soon after the two companions rode out.

"Because that's where I want to go. See how that works, kid? Or do I need your permission now?"

"No, it's just . . . according to this map? It's a straight shot north from the Lazy M to Taos. We have to go west, miles out of our way to reach Santa Fe."

Wild Bill was being even more vigilant than he had on the way down. His penetrating gaze swept the trail on all sides, searching for movements and reflections.

"What about our remounts?" Bill replied. "Or do you want to ride that ornery Old Smoke day and night, wear him down? Maybe get tossed into another cactus patch?"

"Oh, yeah," Josh conceded. "I forgot about the remounts."

"Maybe," Bill suggested, "you wouldn't 'forget' so damn much if you kept your mind on something besides visions of Liddy."

"Easy for *you* to say," Josh shot back. "Women flock to you like flies to syrup."

"That's the cross I bear," Bill replied with a poker face.

"Well, do you have to hog 'em all?"

"Jesus, kid, set it to a tune! Do I look like I been making my living charging stud fees? Besides that pesticatin' Calamity Jane, where's these women flocking all over me?"

"Yeah, but—"

"Yeah, but your ass. Never mind, you hear me? The time to think about women is when you're with them—not when killers are trying to lay a bead on you. I've seen fellows die hard out here because they were stupid enough to daydream and worry when they *shoulda* been keeping their nose to the wind."

Josh knew all this was true. But his jealousy was keen.

"She was starting to like me," he said. "She—"

Bill cut him off, showing a rare streak of exasperation.

"Damn it, Joshua, you're turning into a one-trick pony, you know that? Liddy ain't carrying no brand on her hip. Let the best man win when the time comes. Now put her out of your thoughts and watch for trouble."

Josh said nothing more for the next couple of miles, his face sullen. He had witnessed that intimate little scene, between Liddy and Wild Bill, back at the Lazy M. Women are all the time using *me*, Josh fumed, to goad Wild Bill.

The two horsebackers entered a series of connecting canyons of coarse-grained metamorphic rock. Alternating layers of minerals—feldspar, quartz, mica—gave the rock walls a banded appearance.

It was along this stretch that they had been ambushed on the way down. Bill slid his Winchester '72 repeater from the saddle boot and levered a round into the chamber. He placed the butt plate on his right thigh, ready to fire at a moment's notice.

Josh had gotten over his peeve, ashamed now that Bill had to lecture him like a spoiled child. He, too, forced his senses on the here and now.

However, they reached the outskirts of Santa Fe without incident.

"I've got some quick business at the U.S. Marshals headquarters on Commerce Street," Bill told the kid. "While I'm there, I want you to check all the boardinghouses. Find out if Frank Tutt is staying in Santa Fe. Trouble is, he'd probably use a summer name"—Bill meant an alias—"so go by the description the Chinese kid gave us. I'll meet you at the Frontier Café on College Street."

Josh carried out his orders. But as Bill had feared, nobody had rented a room to anyone named Frank Tutt. Wild Bill was already waiting for him at the Frontier, drinking coffee. As usual, he had taken a table that left his back to a wall and gave him a good view of the entire café.

"No news, Bill," Josh reported, scraping back a chair to join his friend. "If— Man alive!"

Josh had just spotted the five-pointed star pinned to Bill's rawhide vest. "You're a U.S. marshal now!"

"Deputy Marshal, actually. And it's just temporary," Bill assured him. "This is Sam Baxter's badge, Longfellow. I took it off him when we buried him. I had myself deputized like Sam asked me."

"But why?"

"I ain't on Pinkerton's payroll right now, kid. A deputy marshal's pay ain't much. But it's better than working for free. Besides—the days of vigilante justice are behind us. I got no legal authority to get that damn bell back on my own. This way, if somebody carelessly gets himself killed, I won't have to swing for it."

"Is it the bell you want?" Josh asked, confused. "Or Sam Baxter's killer?"

"I got a hunch," Bill replied, "that one comes with the other."

"Marshal Hickok," Josh said, his eyes lighting up. He was already composing a headline, in his mind, for his next far-western dispatch: LEGENDARY GUNMAN PINS ON STAR AGAIN!

"Let's feed our faces, then pick up our remuda and head up to Taos," Bill said, waving the plump Mexican waitress over to their table. "Since Chimayo is right on the trail, we'll stop there quick and see what the priest at El Santuario can tell us. Besides, that's where El Lobo's trail will start. He ain't hauling no seven-hundred-fifty-pound bell around without leaving tracks behind."

From Santa Fe, it was thirty-eight miles to the ill-fated pueblo of Chimayo. The two riders had set out too late to make it by nightfall. When their shadows grew long in the waning sun, they pitched a cold camp beside the trail, using their saddles for pillows. They munched on roast-beef sandwiches made up for them at the café.

They rode into Chimayo about two hours after sunup. The little pueblo seemed just as still and eerie as it had when they rode through three days earlier. White towels still marked dwellings struck by plague.

The two riders moved slowly down the main street, their three remounts trailing behind them on a lead line tied to Wild Bill's saddle horn.

"Why look, Bill!"

Josh pointed toward the brown adobe church at the far end of town. "There's people outside the church. And there's a priest. Nuns, too."

"Wonder why?" Bill said thoughtfully. "It ain't Sunday. Besides, Elena said the church was closed down because of threats from the locals."

Wild Bill and Josh reined in at the church. A small crowd of Mexicans and *indios* watched them from suspicious, fearful eyes. They swung down and threw their bridles, hobbling the horses foreleg to rear with short strips of rawhide.

A short, portly, bald-headed priest in a black cassock stepped forward to greet them. Haggard pockets under his eyes bespoke recent suffering.

"Good morning, Marshal," he said in good, slightly accented English, spotting Wild Bill's badge. "May I help you gentlemen?"

"Maybe you can, Father," Bill greeted him, politely touching the brim of his hat. "I'm guessing you must be Padre Ramon Garcia?"

"*A sus ordenes,*" the priest replied with a slight bow. "At your service. May I ask how you know my name, Marshal?"

"I'm a friend of Elena Vargas. She has explained the situation here."

At this intelligence, Father Garcia flashed a broad smile of welcome.

"Of course! You are Wild Bill Hickok! Elena sent word she was asking you to help us here in Chimayo."

The priest turned away briefly to speak to the fearful-looking crowd, none of whom spoke much English.

"*Es un amigo de Senorita Vargas,*" he explained, and immediately their faces registered smiles of welcome.

"You have arrived just in time, *señors,*" Padre Garcia told them. "Despite the hostility of some here in town, I have decided to open the church briefly for the faithful. Not for mass, just for prayers. Please come in, gentlemen."

"Careful," the priest warned everyone with a smile as he unlocked the heavy front doors. "The thick adobe walls make it much cooler inside. The cool darkness attracts many horned toads, lizards, and rattlesnakes."

He opened the doors and everyone filed inside. The interior was sparse and simple, with an unsanded puncheon floor and raw-lumber pews. Niches in the thick old walls held plaster statues of the beloved saints. Despite the overall simplicity of El Santuario, however, the elaborate altar featured intricate bas-relief designs in hammered gold and silver.

Two black-robed nuns approached the altar and knelt. Bill and Josh watched them, rosaries moving through their fingers as they made novenas. Simply-dressed peons took seats in the pews, saying their beads or praying. One, an old man in dirty work clothes, knelt before the niche containing the statue of San Ysidrio, patron saint of farmers.

"Since our bell was stolen," Padre Garcia explained in a low voice, "seed won't even stay in the ground, much less grow. Wind takes it. Devil Wind, locals call it."

"Padre," Bill said, "I take it that you know the truth about that bell? The truth even Elena doesn't know?"

The priest nodded. "Yes. It may seem inexplicable to outsiders such as yourself. Why, you wonder, would I leave so much gold hanging in a belfry when the residents are so poor and could use the money?"

Bill nodded. "That thought occurred to me," he confessed.

"Whatever its turbulent history, Señor Hickok, that bell arrived in New Spain as a tribute to the greater glory of God. All things are His will, and I had no desire to thwart divine providence. And truly, this church *did* become special to the flock of believers. A 'mother church,' if you will. The terrible misfortunes that have befallen us since the bell was stolen— do they not prove that our bell belongs here, gold or no?"

Despite his skeptical nature, Wild Bill saw plenty of sense in the cleric's remarks. Bill thought of his favorite line from *Hamlet*: "There are more things in heaven and earth, Horatio, than are dreamed of in all your philosophy."

"Elena did tell me," Bill said, "that this place has become famous as a sort of shrine."

"Yes. It is the center for everything that is important to the people: birth, marriage, death.

God, in His infinite wisdom, has sent you, Señor Hickok, to restore El Santuario to us."

Josh shot a malevolent glance at Bill, and Hickok knew why. As a newly appointed deputy marshal, Bill's job—inherited from Sam Baxter—was to turn that golden bell over to the U.S. government, not these poor villagers.

However, Bill left all that alone for now.

"You're sure it was El Lobo who took it?" Hickok asked.

Father Garcia nodded. "I saw him and his men take it. They did it brazenly, in broad daylight. Heavily armed cutthroats no one could challenge. To their credit, they did not blaspheme beyond the crime itself. They terrorized no one and El Lobo let no one steal the altar gold. As he left, he even respectfully begged me to pray for his soul."

"Far as I know, Padre, I've yet to damage any souls. His body is in more danger."

Bill thanked the priest and promised to do what he could to track down the bell. Out behind the church, in the *camposanto* or cemetery, he and Josh found the beginning of the twin ruts that led north toward Taos.

"It's not right, Bill," Josh admonished his mentor. "Leading Padre Garcia on like that, making him think they'll get the bell back. Why didn't you tell him you're working for the government, not the church?"

"And why don't you stick a sock in your big mouth, kid?" Bill replied absently, still staring at the deep ruts. "C'mon, let's hit leather."

While Wild Bill and Josh headed north toward Taos, Frank Tutt was on his way south to find them again.

Hadn't been for that damned Sam Baxter, Frank told himself, Hickok would now be as cold as a fish on ice. But Baxter had paid the ultimate price for being a buttinsky. Frank had not enjoyed killing him—Baxter never did him any wrongs. But when it came to planting Hickok, Frank would shoot the Virgin Mary herself if she got in his line of fire.

Frank was perhaps a half day's ride north of Chimayo. The country hereabouts alternated between prairie-grass flats, when there was standing water, and barren scrub hills when there wasn't.

Plenty of men wanted to plug Hickok. But most of them were motivated by sheer greed for the bounty. Frank, in contrast, meant to settle a blood score. Toward that end, he had been preparing for years. And he had studied Hickok like a text, learning plenty about the enemy he meant to destroy.

Frank's stomach cramped, and he remembered he hadn't eaten since leaving El Lobo's camp near San Juan. Up ahead, perhaps an hour from here, was a crude little *pueblito* called Polvo. There was a fly-blown *cantina* there where a man could get liquor and hot grub, if he didn't mind picking the roaches out of his food.

Frank spurred his *grullo* from a trot to a canter, his thoughts rough and ugly.

"Polvo," Josh said, studying the map spread open across his pommel. "About five miles straight ahead. What's that word mean?"

"Dust," Wild Bill replied. "So don't be expecting no spas. I ain't seen the place for years now. Might have dried up and blowed away since that map was made. If we're lucky, we'll be able to get us some beans and tortillas there."

The two riders found themselves in low hills bristling with creosote, prickly pear, and cholla. A big, glaring sun rode high in the sky, so hot that heat waves made the ground shimmer out ahead of them.

Josh had switched to his favorite horse, his big, well-trained Cavalry sorrel. Since riding out from Chimayo hours earlier, they had passed no one except a few farmers in straw Chihuahua hats, pushing a drove of mules.

Wild Bill spotted a pile of horse droppings and reined in, swinging down to inspect it. He broke it open with the toe of his boot.

"Almost dry inside," he told Josh. "But not quite. In this hot sun, it can't be that old."

Bill's vigilance now impressed Joshua. Every trick Hickok had learned as a scout now came into play. Any man who could drop Sam Baxter was dangerous indeed. And Wild Bill was convinced Frank Tutt still meant to kill him.

They descended from the cactus hills onto a broad expanse of grass. Josh pointed out ahead, his young face squinched up in puzzlement.

"Look there, Bill. There's big circles where the grass has been beaten down. What caused them?"

"Some of the last buffalo herds in the country," Bill explained, "have fled down here to the Southwest. Those are places where mothers of buffalo calves moved round and round during the night to protect the calves from wolves."

About two miles outside the *pueblito* of Polvo, they crossed a high-ground knoll. This was clear, open country with a view for miles.

Again Wild Bill pulled in. To avoid silhouetting himself, Hickok low-crawled to a heap of rocks at the highest point of the knoll. For a long time he studied the landscape, searching for movement.

"Looks empty," he finally reported to Josh.

Before they rode on, both men carefully checked their bits, bridles, girth, latigos, and stirrups. A brief ride brought them into view of a low, log-hut structure with an open cistern dug behind it. It reminded Bill of the posts he used to call stepping-off places because of their location at the edge of the frontier.

Although their stomachs were growling, the horses came first. They dropped the bridles and tethered their mounts and remounts in good graze about twenty yards from the *cantina*. Several more horses, and two mules, were also taking off the grass.

As the two men approached the low building, Bill made sure they stayed clear of the one small window. The hot afternoon was still and quiet except for the hum of cicadas and an occasional voice speaking Spanish from inside.

There was no door, just an old buffalo robe nailed over the entrance. Bill eased it aside to peer inside, Josh watching over his shoulder. The reporter saw a smoky, dark interior with a few crude lumber tables scattered about on a rammed-earth floor.

An Indian wrapped in the traditional *manta* was placing steaming bowls down in front of two Mexicans at one of the tables. A third customer nursed a bottle of tequila at a deal counter. The place was so rustic that hardtack boxes served as chairs.

"It ain't La Fonda," Bill remarked. "But that

119

atole smells pretty good. C'mon, Philly. Let's get outside of some grub."

The two trail-dusty *gringos* stepped inside the smoky interior.

"Welcome, Marshal!" the Pueblo Indian greeted Bill in good English. "Food or liquor?"

"Food first," Bill replied, removing his black hat to slap the dust from it.

Josh was still holding the buffalo hide aside as Bill took off his hat. When his famous golden curls tumbled into view in that clear light, the owner took a second, longer look at the new arrivals. Bill's long gray duster had parted just enough to reveal one of his fancy pearl-handled Peacemakers.

"Tender Virgin!" the Christianized Indian exclaimed. "It is Wild Bill Hickok! *Mamacita!* Señor Hickok, this is a great honor. May I touch you for luck?"

"My pleasure," Bill assured him, stepping forward to give the man a hearty grip.

"I am Antonio Two Moons," the Indian said. "And what is your friend's name?"

Josh had noticed how Indians in New Mexico considered it bad manners to ask a person his name directly, such was the important power of a name. It was the custom to ask a friend instead.

Bill opened his mouth to reply. At that moment, however, a man stepped through the open rear doorway. He was still buttoning his fly after relieving himself at the jakes out back.

Josh took in the lean, young, hard features, all centered on a crooked mouth. The man's eyes registered their presence, and his right hand twitched toward his holster.

But Hickok was faster. Josh never even saw a blur as Bill's Colt cleared the right holster.

"Freeze, Tutt," he commanded in a voice that brooked no debate. "Grab some sky with both hands. You're under arrest for the murder of U.S. Marshal Samuel Baxter. Move one inch, and you'll have a belly full of blue whistlers."

Chapter Ten

Antonio Two Moons and his customers gaped in astonishment. Slowly Frank Tutt brought his hands up over his head. But the smug sneer on his face, Josh thought nervously, implied Tutt was in charge.

"Kiss my lily-white ass, Hickok. What proof you got that I killed anybody?"

"Actually," Bill replied calmly, "none at all—yet. But under Territorial law, proof isn't required to make an arrest. Only for a conviction in court."

Tutt snorted. "And just how do you plan to get me convicted?"

"I don't. But I've got a lot of faith in the power of *ley fuga*."

The sneer bled from Tutt's wire-tight features, replaced by a dark, tight-jawed scowl. Josh had read about the widespread Mexican practice of *ley fuga*, or "flight law." It was the one justifiable case, on the frontier, where men could be shot in the back. According to this practice, widely accepted in the Territories, any prisoner who reportedly tried to flee was to be shot dead on the spot. The assumption was that a fleeing man must be guilty; thus, shooting him saved the tax-payers the cost of jailing, trying, and executing a guilty man.

"Bring your left hand down *slow*," Bill ordered him. "Unbuckle your gunbelt and let it drop. Then give it a good kick toward my partner. Get cute on me, and I'll put an air shaft in you."

Frank did as ordered. Josh scooped up the Colt Navy revolver in its jury-rigged holster.

"Why'n't you just murder me now, big man? Like you back-shot my brother?"

"I killed your piece-of-shit, traitorous brother to his face in a fair fight, Tutt. And if this right now was just *my* business, you'd be carrion by now. I got just one rule when it comes to killing a cockroach like you: Shoot first, ask questions later. But I'm wearing Sam Baxter's badge. And Sam took pride in giving his prisoners a chance, at least, to go back alive."

"Everybody says Wild Bill Hickok is double-rough. To hell with your *ley fuga* and courtrooms. Let's you and me square off in a showdown right now."

Bill shook his head. "Like I told you once, if I didn't have Sam's badge on, it would be done by now. I'd kill you deader than a Paiute grave. But Sam preferred to take his prisoners in. You might call him an idealist."

"That's an excuse, you prettified, perfumed dandy! You got chicken guts, ain'tcha?"

Bill ignored this. He wagged his gun toward the front entrance.

"Outside, mouthpiece. Joshua, dig that short rope out of my right-hand saddlebag, wouldja? We'll tie this jasper's hands up good. Then we'll get his horse."

Instead of going outside, as told, Tutt stood his ground.

"Then at least fight me with your fists, you puffed-up peacock! Or are you afraid to let the world know you're nothing but a weak sister with a phony reputation as a man?"

Bill mulled the fistfight suggestion. No strict law against it, really. And the two men were more or less evenly matched in height and weight, though Tutt was younger by a good ten years, at least.

"All right," Bill agreed. "Let's hug. But no rough-housing in Antonio's place. We'll take it outside."

Hickok kept his gunmetal gaze trained on his prisoner while he spoke to Joshua.

"Kid, get that gunbelt out of reach. Then keep out of my line of fire while you frisk him for hide-out guns or a knife. Tutt, you try anything cute while the kid's patting you down, I'll send you across the Great Divide. You can't move quicker than a bullet."

Josh, stomach tense with nervousness, patted Tutt down quickly. Only later, when it was too late, would he realize he should have been more thorough.

"He's clean," Josh told Bill, stepping back again.

"Outside," Bill ordered again, wagging his Colt.

Tutt emerged into the baking sun of the packed-dirt yard. Antonio Two Moons, the two Mexican customers, and Josh followed him out.

Josh was already holding Tutt's heavy shell belt. Bill unbuckled his and handed it to Antonio, who suddenly looked as if he were holding the Holy Grail. Despite the tension of the moment, Josh had to grin when he saw Antonio swipe a cartridge for luck.

Bill flipped his hat aside, shucked out of his duster and vest, unlooped the buttons of his linen shirt. Tutt, too, peeled off his shirt.

Both men began circling. Josh had never really seen Bill in a hand-to-hand dustup. But it was right here in New Mexico, well before the Civil War, that young Hickok had learned the art of brawling from the likes of Kit Carson and Charlie Bent.

Those Taos trappers were not well-versed in European pugilistics. Rather, they were "thrashers and wrasslers." Tutt, however, was obviously a boxer. The two distinct styles were apparent now as the combatants warily circled. Tutt brought both fists up in front of his face and tucked in his head; Wild Bill held his arms out loosely at his side, ready to grab and throw.

Tutt suddenly jutted in, straight-armed Bill in the lips with his right fist, landed a left hook under his ear. Showing fancy footwork, he danced out of harm's way before Bill could recover.

"S'matter, big man?" Tutt goaded. "You ain't so tough when you have to fight like a man, uh? Don't take no *cojones* to shoot a man in the back like you done my brother."

Bill calmly swiped blood off his mouth with the back of one hand. "You talk too much, Tutt. Your brother was a big talker, too."

"Touch you for luck?" Frank gibed scornfully as

he danced in again and landed a solid blow to Bill's midsection. He followed up with a quick jab that caught the point of Bill's chin.

"*Matelo!*" one of the Mexicans urged Hickok. "Kill him, Wild Bill!"

Tutt swooped in again. This time, however, Bill swept one leg out in a well-timed hook, sweeping Tutt off his feet. He landed hard on his ass. Josh winced when Bill's boot slammed into his face. Tutt sprang back to his feet, spitting chips of broken tooth. Bill caught him with a solid roundhouse right that sent the younger man staggering again.

Suddenly Tutt had lost interest in goading his opponent. As he got up again, Josh saw his hand slip quickly into a front pocket of his trousers. When it emerged, the knuckles were lethally wrapped with Tutt's "drinking jewelry"—heavy horseshoe nails welded together.

"Bill!" Josh warned. "Watch out! He—"

Josh was too late. Tutt's steel-wrapped fist slammed hard into the vulnerable point of the jaw halfway between the ear and the chin. Wild Bill's knees folded like an empty sack, and he flopped face-first into the dirt, knocked senseless.

Josh, whey-faced, clawed for the pinfire revolver in its chamois holster under his armpit. But Frank Tutt had the reflexes of a puma cat. He grabbed his gunbelt off Josh's shoulder and knocked the reporter ass-over-applecart into the dirt beside Bill.

But Josh knew he couldn't let up, or Tutt would get his gun out of the holster. The youth got his weapon out and came up to his feet again, cocking his LeFaucheux.

Tutt lifted his left foot, touched a spot by the heel, and a five-inch steel blade shot out from the front of the thick sole! Josh had no time to react before the blade punched hard into the meaty heel of his right palm.

Fire leaped up Josh's arm, and his revolver flew into the dirt. Tutt obviously intended to shoot Hickok. But one of the Mexicans saved the day, producing an old over-and-under dragoon pistol from beneath his *manta*. The gun's booming roar made everybody's ears ring.

Unfortunately for all but Tutt, the big, half-ounce ball missed by a cat's whisker. But at least it scared Tutt into flight. He raced back through the log hovel to his *grullo*, tethered in grass out back.

"See you in hell, Hickok!" came his taunting shout. Moments later ironclad hooves could be heard, pounding out across the flats.

"Well, kid," Wild Bill said grimly as he unwrapped Josh's wounded hand. "Tutt took that trick. I see now he's twice the trouble his brother Dave was."

Bill had been out cold for nearly ten minutes. Now his left jaw was swollen, turning the dark purple of grapes. Antonio had quickly wrapped Josh's copiously bleeding hand in bandage cloth. But that blade had gone in deep, all the way to bone, and Bill knew from experience the bleeding wouldn't stop on its own.

"You saved my bacon, Longfellow," Bill added, speaking through swollen, bloody lips. "You're a damn good man to ride the river with."

Despite the horrid, throbbing pain, Josh swelled with pride. Frontiersmen like Wild Bill Hickok did not lightly dole out such praise.

"Unfortunately," Bill also told him, "you're going to bleed to death if we don't cauterize this.

It's going to hurt, kid. Hurt like the dickens. But I'll do it quick."

"Antonio?"

"*Sí*, Señor Wild Bill?"

"Go inside and build up a fire in the stove, wouldja? And fetch us a bottle of strong liquor. *Pulque*, if you got any."

"Right away."

Antonio started to go inside, then paused to say from the doorway:

"That man was a coward. He could not beat you, Wild Bill, with his bare hands. He had to cheat."

"Oh, he cheated, all right. But you see, Antonio, it was *my* job to expect he'd cheat. So the truth is, he was the better man—that time." Bill added in his quiet, genial way, "But what's done today can be undone tomorrow."

"I only wish you had shot him on sight," Antonio added. "*Al infierno con ley fuga*. To hell with flight law!"

"He's right," Bill told Josh. "Out of respect to Sam, I tried to go by the book. Almost got both of us killed. From here on out, it's the Code of Hickok."

Bill led Josh back inside and made him sit down. While Josh choked down as much *pulque*—a milky, strong cactus liquor—as he could, Wild Bill thrust the iron blade of his knife into the glowing coals of the stove.

He handed Josh his leather belt. "Bite down on that, Longfellow. Then stare at the painting behind you—the one of the naked lady."

There was no painting behind Josh, naked ladies or anything else. But when the curious reporter turned to look, distracted, Wild Bill quickly seized his arm. He laid the red-hot blade against the kid's mangled hand.

There was a sound—and a smell—like meat sizzling in fat. Josh's entire body tried to shoot up off the seat, but Wild Bill held him down. The kid's scream of pain was so bloodcurdling, Antonio and the Mexicans all made the sign of the cross.

The kid slumped over the table, passing out. But when Bill finally removed the glowing blade, the edges of the wound had sealed together. It would leave a hell of an ugly scar. However, the bleeding had stopped.

Antonio brought in some gentian root paste to soothe the ravaged flesh. Bill smeared plenty on, then wrapped the kid's hand again.

When Josh started to groan, coming to, Bill managed to pour more *pulque* down his throat. Better to get him drunk and let him sleep awhile. Bill had once cauterized his own wounds after a grizzly bear ripped him up in an attack at Raton Pass. There was no pain on earth quite like the aftermath of a cauterizing.

While the kid slept, Bill went outside and followed Frank Tutt's trail far enough to see where he was headed. After fleeing due east, the trail doubled back to the northwest.

Toward Taos. Meaning Tutt was probably going to make a report to El Lobo.

"All right, then, Mr. Tutt," Bill muttered as he reined his chestnut back toward Polvo. "Like you said—see you in hell."

"Easy . . . *easy*, there!" shouted El Lobo Flaco as his men struggled to lift the golden bell out of the buckboard. *"Cuidado!* Careful with it! Do not

129

chip off the coating paint. I want no one to see what is underneath it."

Several Apaches and Mexicans, muscles straining like tent ropes in a storm wind, eased the bell out of its buckboard and into an open boxcar. They worked by moonlight to minimize attention to their task. Those who were not lifting stood guard, heavily armed. Several wore crossed bandoliers bristling with ammunition.

The adobe pueblo of Taos was dark and silent except for generous moonlight and a lonely dog that howled irregularly, somewhere out beyond the train siding. Witter Boyd himself, owner of the private narrow-gauge railroad line, would be driving the locomotive. Right now Witter was building up a head of steam for the forty-mile night run, due east, to Springer. Witter meant to highball it, wide open all the way, pushing thirty miles per hour and praying nobody had torn out tracks to derail them.

The buckboard rose noticeably on its leaf springs when the bell had been off-loaded.

"Benito!" El Lobo called to one of his men.

"*Sí, Jefe!*"

"Load one buckboard onto the train with the bell. We will need it, once we arrive in Springer, for the trip south to Cerrillos."

"*Sí, Jefe.* And the fodder wagon?"

El Lobo eased his lips away from his teeth, his face sinister and dangerous and ghostly in that bluish moonlight.

"I want all of you to fill it with rocks. Many rocks, enough to weight it down as the bell did. Then pick one man to stay behind. Early in the morning, hire a young boy from the public square. Pay him generously to drive those rocks *straight north* toward the Colorado border."

Benito, too, grinned as he caught on. "Toward Pueblo and the big smelter there, *verdad*?"

El Lobo nodded. "It will leave deep ruts. Anyone following will think we are taking the bell north to melt it down. Meantime, we will be heading south to the smelter at Cerrillos. And we have some additional freight I need to show you. Witter is kindly letting us use it."

El Lobo hopped into the boxcar and tugged a dirty piece of canvas aside.

"Virgin de Guadalupe," Benito muttered. He gaped at the ten-barreled Gatling gun. The hopper that stored and fed shells was already attached. A metal ammo crate sat under the gun.

"You know how to use it?" El Lobo demanded.

Benito nodded. "I had one that I stole from drunk *Tejanos*. A child could fire it."

A rider approached from the darkness beyond the train, and a half-dozen weapons came up to the ready. El Lobo covered the gun and backed away from it. But he remained on the boxcar.

"Hallo!" Tutt's voice rang out. "Hold your fire, boys!"

Tutt, his *grullo* badly lathered, rode right up to the tracks. Sitting in his saddle, he was at eye level with his boss.

"Hickok's for sure coming," Tutt reported. "And he's wearing a star. He damn near arrested me at Polvo."

"Coming when? Now, you mean?"

Frank shook his head. "I watched my backtrail good. More likely, tomorrow morning. I cut up his partner pretty good, it'll slow them down. I

131

rode full bore to get here, and I took the shortcut through Arroyo Hondo."

El Lobo relaxed a little. His eyes flicked to the covered Gatling gun. " 'Sta bien. Let Hickok come. If all goes well, he will soon be riding in the opposite direction from us. You wait here, Frank. Stay on Hickok like black on night."

"Oh, I intend to, boss. Hickok is my favorite boy now. I damn near did for his ass in Polvo. Next time I brace that prissy, he's going under."

Chapter Eleven

Even as a yellow-orange ball of sun broke over the eastern horizon, Wild Bill and Josh rode into the deserted center of Taos plaza.

"Why, look!" Josh exclaimed.

He pointed with his bandaged hand toward a tall cottonwood pole erected in the center of the plaza. The American flag fluttered in a gentle breeze.

"That's downright disrespectful to our flag," Josh complained. "It must have been left flying all night. The flag is supposed to be lowered before dark."

Bill chuckled. "Don't get your pennies in a bunch, patriot. Thanks to Kit Carson and some others, Taos plaza is one of the few places where the American flag can legally fly day and night."

"Why?"

"Back in '61, just before the Great War, there were Confederate sympathizers around here who kept trying to haul down the Union standard and fly the rebel flag in its place. But that didn't sit too well with Kit, Captain Smith Simpson, and some others. So they *nailed* the Stars and Bars to that pole. Then they went right over there . . ."

Bill pointed to where St. Vrain's General Store once stood, on the south side of the plaza. "And they stood guard. That flag's been waving up there ever since. Only lowered and replaced when it's weather-tattered."

"Man alive! That story's going in my next dispatch," Josh vowed, impressed.

Taos Pueblo itself, however, was a bit less than impressive. Mostly drab adobe buildings with batten shutters instead of glass windows. Nonetheless, Josh gazed around in awe at this rustic, yet historic, place. Its roots gave America a long history. Many even believed the name Taos reflected the fact that its first ancient settlers came from north China, followers of the great master Lao-tze and his doctrine of Taoism.

It wasn't history, however, that Wild Bill was in search of now. For a long time, he studied everything with the alert vigilance of an animal in new territory. Then, reassured, he turned his bruised and battered face toward the twin ruts they had been following since they left Chimayo the day before.

The ruts evidently continued north of the pueblo. But Bill reined in where the tracks swerved in close to the old train yard at the edge of town.

Both riders swung down, Josh favoring his throbbing right hand. An old, diamond-stack steam locomotive with a single boxcar attached was parked on the narrow-gauge siding.

Bill studied the ruts for some time while the

new sun heated up the day. Josh watched him glance inside the empty boxcar. Then he walked up front and laid his hand on one of the locomotive's steam vents.

"Still warm," Wild Bill muttered. "Should be cool if it sat all night. Still a horse smell in the boxcar, too."

Josh didn't understand Bill's drift. "But the trail continues on to the north," he pointed out. "Toward Pueblo, Colorado. You said that's a mining town. They could smelt gold there."

"That's what we're s'posed to conclude," Wild Bill agreed. "But then why did El Lobo bother to swing in so close to the rails?"

"You're thinking they loaded the bell, and everything else, onto the train and took it east?"

"The way you say," Bill replied. "Be a mite crowded, but with a few men riding in the steam engine, they could do it."

He glanced toward a little canvas-and-clapboard structure in the middle of the train yard. A horse tethered beside it suggested someone lived there.

"It's early to come calling," Wild Bill said. "We'll feed our faces first."

The two men shared a can of tomatoes and the last of their hardtack. Then Josh built a fire right beside the tracks and boiled a handful of coffee beans. By the time they finished their leisurely meal, the streets of Taos were beginning to fill and thicken.

Josh was scrubbing the coffeepot out with sand when someone inside the little shanty began singing in a gravelly voice:

> *And the moonbeams lit*
> *on the tipple of her nit . . .*

Bill walked over to the little shanty.

"Hallo!" he called out.

A man threw back the old moth-eaten blanket that served as an entrance flap. He was perhaps fifty or so, portly but not fat, with deep-sunk eyes like a pair of wounds. He wore old stovepipe trousers, and shaving soap mottled his face.

"Howzit goin'?" Bill greeted him.

"Same shit, different day, Marshal."

"The boss around?"

The man gave them a friendly, snaggle-toothed grin. "Believe it or not, fellas, I'm the big chief around here. Witter Boyd's the name. C'mon in and have a seat. Place is humble, but me and the cooties like it."

"Humble" was an understatement, Josh quickly saw. Two cowhide-covered chairs, a packing-crate table, and a shakedown of dirty straw in one corner, obviously the bed. A coal-oil lamp gave off a pungent stench.

A fragment of mirror was nailed to one wall. Witter resumed his task of scraping off whiskers with a straight razor.

His eyes cut to Wild Bill's battered face, then Josh's bandage. "If you two was the winners, Marshal, I'd shorely hate to see the losers."

Bill grinned, for Witter himself had a cauliflower ear from too many blows in his youth.

"I'm on the trail of a man called El Lobo Flaco," Hickok informed him. "Seen him lately?"

"Seen *him*? Huh! I'd sooner run into a she-grizz with cubs. That El Lobo is meaner than Satan with a sunburn."

Boyd tapped a finger against his temple. "You ask me, I don't think all his biscuits're done, neither. Sumbitch is crazy."

"Make a run last night with your train?" Bill asked casually.

"Naw, hell no. I never make night runs on accounta there's still Apache renegades in these parts. Old Bessie ain't been fired up since she hauled a load of longhorn cattle to the terminal in Springer. Butcher beef bound for a rez up north. That was day before yestiddy."

Josh expected Wild Bill to challenge this, invoking the authority of his badge. But he only nodded. " 'Preciate your time, Mr. Boyd."

Before the two visitors left, Boyd remarked: "Only a soft-brained fool would go after the Skinny Wolf without a small army. He's got tough riders with him at all times. Killers all. Apaches and Mexer soldiers what deserted."

Boyd's manner was relaxed and conversational. But Josh had the distinct impression they'd just been warned. Bill thanked him and they left.

"Kid," Bill remarked as they swung up into leather, "Witter Boyd is affable enough. But I'd say he's the best liar since Simon Peter denied Christ."

"He's crooked, huh?"

"Crooked as cat shit. He took Lobo, his gang, and that bell to Springer last night. But I know his type—he won't admit anything even if we carve an eye out of him. He's tough as boar bristles."

"But why Springer?"

"That's one nut we ain't cracked yet," Bill admitted, reining his mount around toward the center of town. "There's no smelter in Springer— it's just a little crossroads stop. But see, it would be a good move to throw anybody off your trail. There *is* a smelter down south of Springer, down in Cerrillos."

"So are we riding to Springer?"

Bill shook his head. "Not if I can avoid it. It's forty miles with no water. There *used* to be a U.S. Army remount station there with a telegraph. We can go to the Western Union and send a telegram. Verify which direction El Lobo's trail goes. If it's to the south, then we'll know for certain it's Cerrillos. Save us a day and a night's ride."

"Good. I'll file my next story after you send your telegram."

"You mind reading it to me first, Longfellow?"

"Sure. I didn't say anything about the gold bell, just like you asked."

Josh pulled the story out of his pocket and read it while the two men rode. As Josh had promised, most of it was a stirring tribute to Sam Baxter, with Wild Bill as his principal source.

"Kid," Bill marveled when Josh fell silent, "you're some pumpkins as a writer. Look there, you gave me goose bumps. But Allan Pinkerton's going to have a cow when he reads it. I took French leave from his agency, and here I'm pinning on a badge for half the money."

By now Taos was much busier than when they rode in. Josh saw Indians at work grinding corn and tanning hides. But the two riders were in for disappointment: The Western Union office was deserted, evidently gutted by a recent fire.

"What now?" Josh demanded. "We have to ride all the way to Springer?"

Bill shook his head. "Maybe not, slick. I got one more ace up my sleeve. C'mon. And keep your eyes peeled for trouble."

* * *

Bill followed the telegraph line out of town. He reined in about a mile south of Taos Pueblo. The first thing he did was make sure the rimrock was well off in the distance, minimizing ambush chances.

"Light down, Longfellow," Bill told Josh, swinging to the ground and digging into a saddle pocket. "I want you to hand me this after I get started up that pole."

"What's *that?*" Josh demanded, staring at the small battery Bill pulled out. It was attached by colored wires to some kind of switch.

"It's called a pocket relay, kid. I took it out of Sam's saddlebag. All U.S. marshals carry one; so do most Cavalry units. You cut the main wires and fasten the pocket relay to the cut ends. Then you can send or receive Morse to the nearest telegraph station that's up and operating. For us, on this line, that should mean Springer."

"You know how to tap out Morse code, Wild Bill?"

Hickok, showing good agility, was already skinning up the pole.

"I hope I still remember enough to make sense. All us deputies had to know it. Been a while, though. Hand me the relay, kid."

Josh had put his derby away earlier. He wore a military cap with a havelock to protect the back of his neck from the unrelenting sun. It tickled his neck now as he reached up, handing Bill the device.

Hickok climbed up to the wire and cut it with his knife. Josh watched the frontiersman, brows touching in a frown of concentration, splice the main wire to the relay. Then he worked the sender in a series of pulses and pauses.

Some time passed in silence.

"Cross your fingers," Hickok called down. "The wire could be down somewhere. Or the battery might be too weak. Or maybe there's nobody there to receive the mes— *Whoa!*"

Bill fell silent as a message abruptly came pulsing back. Hickok sounded it out.

"Affirmative on arrival . . . of El Lobo . . . bearing south . . . too many for me to handle . . . have requested help from Fort Union . . . use extreme caution, stop."

"Must be the U.S. marshal there," Bill said.

"Good work!" Josh praised. "But now what?"

Wild Bill, grinning in triumph, was busy unfastening the pocket relay from the main wire.

"Kid, they've *got* to be headed toward Cerrillos. Nothing else down that way. Now we've saved forty miles. That means we can get in to good position just east of Pecos at a spot called Chama Bluffs. It's high ground, excellent firing position. I once held off Dan Turner's gang from there."

"But what about that help from Fort Union? The—"

"Out here, you save *your own* ass. Even if the fort does respond, they'll be half a day staging the patrol. Forget the Army. You're a literate man— what's Mr. Emerson's greatest essay?"

" 'Self-reliance,' " Josh admitted.

"Damn straight."

Wild Bill was still about ten feet above the ground when a fist-size chunk of wood flew from the pole. A fractional second later, a rifle shot shattered the hot stillness.

"God kiss me!" Bill sang out even as splinters pecked at his face.

Hickok didn't bother climbing the rest of the way. The relay unit almost banged off Josh's head when Bill dropped it. Hickok himself fell right behind it, landing in a crouch.

Again, again, yet again the hidden weapon spoke its deadly piece. Bullets *whump*ed into the ground, sending up geysers of dirt.

"Cover down under your remount!" Bill ordered Josh, for there was absolutely no natural ground cover around them. "But move *quick* if the horse is shot."

Bill himself, however, ran a zigzag pattern into the open. Sliding the Winchester '72 from its saddle boot, Bill tucked and rolled just in time to avoid the next bullet.

"I figured Tutt was notching his sight on me," Bill told Josh, rolling immediately to a new position. "That's why I kept us well out in the open flats. He's *got* to have a scope at this range."

Josh, his lips chapped with fear, realized what Bill was doing, even as Hickok rolled from spot to spot to throw off Tutt's aim. Hickok was "following the bullet back to the gun," as he called it. He was using strike angles, and an expert instinct for ballistics, to locate the shooter's probable position.

"Gotta be it," he muttered, swinging the Winchester's muzzle onto a beadline with a tumble of glacial moraine dead ahead. With no specific target, Bill emptied the repeater in a saturation volley.

Bill worked the lever again and again; shell casings winked in the sunlight as they were ejected, and the acrid stink of spent powder stained the air. Either Tutt had already left, or Bill's wall of lead sent him packing. At any rate, the sniping ceased for now.

"Let's ride, kid," Bill called out, rising to catch his chestnut. "Tutt will have to wait. If we let El Lobo and his bunch get that bell past Chama Bluffs, it's as good as gone."

Calamity Jane emitted a screeching roar that combined a Sioux war cry with the kill cry of a puma. At the sound, a dozen galloping camels broke their line formation to form a flying wedge. They left Ignatius, the master camel that Jane rode, at the point position.

"Well, God a'mighty!" Jane roared out with an ear-to-ear grin. "You ugly flea traps finally done it right, huh?"

Jane pulled in and fed a stale biscuit to each animal to reward it. Jane had the herd well east of the Lazy M, teaching the camels to hold standard Cavalry battle formations in the arid flatland.

Jane was about to climb aboard Ignatius again when she spotted them: several flashes of light from the Indian mirror station at Black Mesa, north of here. She glanced south and also saw answering flashes from the village at Point Otero.

Jane couldn't read the actual messages. But so much mirror activity usually meant trouble for somebody. And with Wild Bill Hickok in the area, chances were good the trouble involved him. That seemed a law of nature.

"Bill's up against it, Ignatius," Jane told her favorite. "And the trouble's coming our way. We got to be ready. Anybody even touches a curl on Bill's head, I'll cut 'em open from neck to nuts!"

Jane brought her light sisal whip across the

ugly beast's neck, and he obediently knelt so she could climb on.

"By grab!" Calamity Jane cried out. "Uncle Sam's Humpback Battalion will soon see their first combat action!"

Chapter Twelve

"That's where we hole up, Longfellow," Wild Bill announced as the two riders topped a long rise. "Chama Bluffs. Some call it Battle Bluffs, been so many scrapes there."

It was all laid out in front of them like an artillery map. On the long western boundary ran the Rio Chama, fairly narrow hereabouts but hemmed in by steep, stony banks. To the east was a series of connecting redrock canyons, impassable for any conveyance. The only way past these twin obstacles was a narrow, grassy draw that led to the south.

Bill said, "If anybody's looking to get somewheres south of here, like Cerrillos, either they pass the bluffs or they go four days out of the way."

Bill pointed again. "See how the bluffs stick way out into the draw?" he said. "Leaves only about twenty yards of clear ground before you drop plumb into the canyons. Sorta 'funnels' anyone trying to pass, forces them in close to the base of the bluffs. Directly into the line of fire from above."

Bill was speaking from experience here, not battle strategy. Josh paid close attention, getting it all straight in his mind now while he was still fairly calm. He had survived other hard stands at Wild Bill's side, so he knew that, soon, quick reactions, rigid discipline, and heroic exertion must replace thinking and planning.

"The bluffs got one major weakness," Bill conceded as they rode closer to the headland, leading their remuda. "It's just a steep, grassy slope up to the rocks where we'll be. It's high up, but it ain't that hard for attackers to climb unless there's constant firepower from above."

Josh understood Bill's grim point. "Constant firepower" was beyond their capability. Josh had only six cartridges left, and this time Bill couldn't chew him out for negligence. Pinfires were hard to find outside of big cities like Denver. And Bill had been in an all-fired hurry to leave, giving Josh no chance to stock up.

As for Bill: He had enough ammo on him for the usual defensive purposes. But he was understocked for a siege. Besides the twelve loads always ready in his Colts, day or night, he had less than a third of a box of .44 cartridges left, about twenty shells, to share between rifle and short guns.

Luckily, Bill was able to buy an old breechloader from a retired soldier who ran the ferry at Rio Moro. It was a cap-and-ball single-shot rifle made by William F. Marston of New York City. Although more than twenty years old now, this was to be Josh's "main siege weapon," as Bill put it, with his pinfire reserved for close-in charges.

Now, as the two men led their mounts up the steep front slope of Chama Bluffs, Josh could feel the heavy cartridge pouch swinging at his waist. Bill was about to give him a quick lesson in firing the antiquated weapon.

"That old percussion gun is slow against charges," Bill conceded. "And your wounded hand will slow you down more. But a Marston rifle always has an excellent ramp sight on it, makes it an accurate piece. Accuracy's important, Longfellow, when you're outnumbered and slowed down. No more 'saturation volleys' like I fired at Frank Tutt back near Taos. It's down to the Lakota battle slogan: One bullet, one enemy."

However, their first priority, once atop the bluffs, was to move the horses all the way back clear of the line of fire. They tethered each animal in good graze.

"They need rubdowns. But they're safe now unless attackers breach that slope in front of us," Bill reminded Josh. "We can't let that happen. And don't forget—it ain't just the Skinny Wolf and his bootlickers we got to watch for. Frank Tutt's out there somewhere, too, nursing a bad grudge."

Bill's serious tone made Josh carefully study the terrain below, once they'd returned to the vulnerable front of the bluffs. The only movements he could detect, however, were cloud shadows sliding across the scrub flats.

Quickly, Bill showed Josh how to charge and fire the old breechloader.

"Just chew open the cardboard cartridge," Bill said, spitting out a wad of brown paper, "and thumb the ball through the loading gate, right there. Then you just stick the rest of the cartridge in, like so, close the breech, and your primer's built into that leather base on the cartridge."

Bill thumbed the hammer to full cock and handed Josh the weapon.

"It's got a long trigger pull. Fire it once to check your battle sights and get the feel."

Bill pointed toward a heart-shaped boulder about two hundred yards out into the draw. "Aim dead center on that rock. Remember to squ*eeee*ze that trigger gradual—don't jerk it and buck your aim."

Josh's wounded hand made it difficult to grip the wood stock securely. But his thumb and fingers were free of bandages. Finally, the old rifle kicked hard into his shoulder. Below, a spray of rock dust shot up from the designated target.

"Not bad," Bill praised. His own Winchester was propped against a nearby boulder. "Low and to the left. So raise the rear sight a click or two, and tend to lead right when you shoot at moving targets."

Josh did as told, his stomach nervous but his hands steady. Hickok, meantime, kept his gunmetal eyes in constant motion, watching the approach below.

"Bill?"

"Hmm?"

"It just sank through to me," Josh admitted. "Now that we're up here to stay, we're sort of . . . trapped. I mean, either we win or we die, there's no retreating?"

Bill nodded. "That rings right. We've got to play this game through, kid. You sure you want a story this bad? You're free to leave, but you'd best do it quick."

Josh's mouth felt stuffed with cotton. But he managed to answer. "It ain't just the story, though that's important. It's just . . . I'm your partner. A man doesn't desert his partner, not out west. It just ain't done, not if a man wants to look himself in the eye ever again."

Hickok looked at the kid, admiration clear in his eyes.

"By God, you *have* learned something since high school, haven't you? But you may regret it yet, Joshua. Now, clear out your head of them lofty ideas and get your thoughts bloody. We got a set-to coming."

"God a'mighty! I know where Wild Bill would go in a hard fight."

Chama Bluffs, Jane told herself. Any set-piece battle in these parts ended up at the bluffs. Wild Bill had defended that position before, taking out three of Turner's gang and wounding two more before they retreated. Bill got shot, too, but his thick leather belt kept the hole shallow.

Jane's Humpback Battalion were performing flawlessly. Right now, as they loped in a skirmish line, they held precise alignment like the best-trained regimental horses. It was as if they sensed the fight coming, and their cantankerous natures longed for the conflict.

However, Jane was still well south of the bluffs when she heard it: the first rifle cracks echoing across the open lowland. And amazingly, the clear, mellow, reverberating ring of a bell!

"Haul ass, Ignatius!" Jane urged her ugly steed, leaning far forward to speak lovey phrases into his wrinkled ear. She pulled the long-barreled

Smith & Wesson from her bright red sash and waved it over her head like a battle guidon.

"My Bill's in the thick of it, darlin's! Anybody ever kills that purty critter, it'll be *me*. Haw! Gee up, Ignatius! We got to settle some hash!"

"Hijo de puta," El Lobo swore in his low, whispering voice. Jemez had just returned with the news that Hickok had taken up a position on Chama Bluffs. "Just the two of them, you say?"

The Apache nodded. These hair-face idiots, he thought, always waste words on what is obvious and has been said once already. Only women and children wasted talk.

El Lobo glanced over his shoulder, into the bed of the buckboard. Between the bell and the box seat, a piece of ratty canvas covered the Gatling gun. Hickok must not know they had a Gatling. Not even a fool would try to hold those bluffs against eleven riders with firepower like that.

"Benito!" he shouted.

"Sí, Jefe?"

"Get into the buckboard. Fill the hopper with shells. Then cover the gun again. Wait until my command. Then uncover the gun and rain hell on Hickok!"

"Sí, Jefe."

"Jemez!" El Lobo called to the leader of the Apache renegades. "I want you on point. Two of your men wide on each flank. Diego!"

One of the Mexican riders responded.

"Diego, I want you, Juan, Paco, and Javier in a tight ring around the buckboard. Benito showed all of you how to crank and aim the gun. Any questions? No? All right then. If Benito gets shot, one of you takes over immediately. I don't want that gun falling silent until all of you are dead."

"Nine . . . ten . . . eleven of them," Bill finally confirmed, watching the riders approach below. "Eleven we can see, anyhow."

Josh knew Bill meant Frank Tutt, who made it an even dozen, although it wasn't clear where he was right now. Bill's theory held that Tutt was holding back to see how El Lobo's gang fared.

"Christ, they ain't even troubling to slow down," Bill complained as he threw his Winchester into his shoulder. "They know we're up here, and they don't give a tinker's damn. We'll see if this slows 'em down."

Bill steadied the repeater's barrel on a boulder, laying the notch sight center of mass on the bone breastplate of one of the Apaches. The Winchester kicked, and the slug, arcing a bit high, punched through the Indian's throat. The bullet not only knocked him from the saddle—it still had enough force to ring the bell smartly as it ricocheted off.

"Target!" Josh exclaimed, as he had heard Bill do before in a gunfight. "Good one!"

"Little high," Bill muttered, his vanity wounded even in the face of death. If they survived this, the kid would describe that sloppy shot for all to read.

"Joshua, take out the team on that buckboard! We got to slow 'em down, or they'll be past the draw in two shakes!"

Joshua began laying down his bead even as Bill shot a second Apache off his mount. But before Josh could take up the endless trigger slack, all hell broke loose below.

That Gatling opened up with hellish fury, a stuttering and shattering burst of fire. In an eyeblink, bullets were thumping in on their position nineteen to the dozen. Besides the deadly lead itself, the bullets sent up a dangerous spray of flying debris. In seconds, both defenders' faces were pocked with small, bleeding cuts.

No science to it—that Gatling clearly and dramatically cut down on the time either man dared expose himself to fire while aiming. El Lobo brilliantly seized the advantage: With the Gatling still stuttering behind him, and the two men above still shaken, he sent four men rushing up the front slope.

"Team!" Wild Bill repeated frantically to the cowering Josh. "Nerve up! Shoot the team! We got to slow that buckboard!"

Bill himself had an even greater priority to shoot. He recklessly rolled out from cover, braving a windstorm of bullets pounding in at the rate of 750 per minute. He levered his Winchester and fired on the roll, dropping one of the Mexicans who was advancing up the slope. Again Bill rolled, levered, came up briefly to shoot, and knocked a second man from the saddle.

This broke the charge and sent the other two riders back to join the main formation. Bill, scuttling crab-fashion, rushed back toward cover. Josh, meantime, entrusted his soul to God Almighty and raised his old breechloader even as shells hummed and whiffed past his ears. Bill's crazy rush had fired him up.

There were four horses in the traces. Josh sighted on the right front animal, shooting at the bay's heaving flank. A puff of dust sprang up when the bullet struck well behind the shoulder.

A thin rope of blood spurted out, and the animal staggered, then lurched to a halt.

There were two immediate results of Josh's single, well-placed shot: the buckboard, too, lurched hard, throwing the gun's aim off the men above, and the conveyance came nearly to a stop, the dying horse all but braking the others.

"Good shot, but damn it, gloat later, kid! Recharge that piece!" Wild Bill admonished the gaping youth. "I count seven of 'em still alive, and they look more pissed off than scared."

"Six!" Bill amended a moment later as he blew a flank rider in a splaying heap to the ground. The acrid stench of gunpowder hovered in a blue cloud over their position. Josh felt his ears still ringing from the Gatling burst.

Josh was frantically chewing open a cartridge when Bill suddenly slapped the Winchester into the youth's hands.

"Never mind that old gun, kid. We got to stop that Gatling before they open up again. I'm rushing their position. Here."

About ten shells clinked into the grass beside Josh. "It's up to you, slick. Keep that air whistling down there without hitting me. You're the only cover I got."

Josh glanced below. The skinny man in the shako hat, probably El Lobo, was frantically helping another man realign the Gatling. The others kept a lively wall of slugs whanging in on the nest of rocks where Bill and Josh were pinned down.

"Bill, are you crazy? There's too many, they'll kill you!"

"Crazy is exactly what it is, kid, so it just might work. Crazy is never in their battle plans. With odds like this, and that damn gun, we won't survive on the defensive. Now listen. The very second I hit that slope, you start peppering them. Make it lively, mister! Don't let up until you're out of ammo. Now!"

Wild Bill didn't even try to run down that dangerous, exposed, precipitous slope. Instead, he simply hurled himself out in a somersault and started literally tumbling down the grass like a loosened boulder.

The rest happened so quickly that only later, when Josh recounted it for millions of American readers, could he sort it out.

Despite his throbbing hand wound, Josh smoothly levered and fired the Winchester, keeping the heat off Wild Bill for those first moments. When Bill's wild tumbling and rolling body was perhaps halfway down the slope, the Gatling opened up on him.

Josh watched divots of grass fly all around Bill as shells chunked and thumped in near him. Josh sent two shells into the back of the wagon, making the gunner duck for a moment.

Bill thumped to a stop, came up dizzy and disoriented, but with a short iron in each fist. Josh was out of shells now, down to his pinfire revolver—useless at this range. His jaw dropped in pure astonishment as Hickok stood up tall, guns blazing in the face of certain death.

El Lobo had leaped behind the bell. Bill's first shot opened a neat hole in Benito's forehead, and he slumped dead over the Gatling.

Still standing in the open, Wild Bill's clothing and hair actually flapped like a storm flag as the five survivors threw lead at him. Bill's Colts blazed and Josh watched one, two, three men die quicker than he could swallow his amazement.

It was down to El Lobo and one of the Apaches. But Bill's Colts fell silent, and Josh knew the gutsy frontiersman was out of ammo. Josh was frantically recharging the breechloader, even as Bill drew his knife and rushed the Indian, steeling his muscles for the leap.

Josh saw a brief, frantic struggle of thrashing limbs. Bill's knife hand moved up and down in several vicious stabs, the blade turning red in that merciless, glaring sun. But El Lobo had moved in, six-shooter aimed at the struggling Hickok point blank. And Josh, hands clumsy and trembling now, would never get reloaded in time!

But in that racket of blazing guns, shouting men, and frantically crying horses, Josh had not heard another noise, approaching from the south of the bluffs: the thunder of charging hooves.

"Hii-ya! Hii-ya!"

Calamity Jane, yipping the fierce war cry of the Northern Cheyenne, came flying around the shoulder of Chama Bluffs, bouncing on the uneven back of Ignatius. Her camel battalion, braying raucously, surrounded her.

Calamity Jane was the second-best female shootist in America, bested only by the young phenomenon Annie Oakley. Even as El Lobo took up his trigger slack to kill Hickok, Jane's Smith & Wesson spat an orange streak of muzzle fire. Her bullet punched the shako hat off El Lobo's head— and took the top of his skull with it.

Josh ran blindly down the slope, tripping several times before he reached the draw below. Dead men lay sprawled everywhere.

Bill, exhausted, sides heaving, lay in the grass beside the Apache he had just killed. El Lobo's body lay only a few feet away.

Jane dismounted and knelt beside her blond hero. His bloodied and bruised face flashed her a weak but grateful smile.

"What's cookin', good-lookin'?" Jane greeted him with her gap-toothed grin.

Josh rapped the big bell a good one with his knuckles, making it ring a little.

"We got it, Bill," he said triumphantly. "And El Lobo's worm fodder. You completed Marshal Baxter's last mission."

But Josh knew they couldn't breathe easy just yet—not with Frank Tutt out there somewhere, obsessed with vengeance.

"Fun," Josh heard Wild Bill mutter before he passed out. "That's why I came down here. Get some goddamn *fun*."

Chapter Thirteen

As Josh had suggested they might, the Cavalry did finally arrive, alerted by the U.S. marshal at Springer station. But just as Bill predicted: The soldiers arrived too late to offer any combat assistance.

In fact, their horses went loco on them the moment they spotted the camels, scattering to the four directions. Only when Jane had driven her spitting, foreign-smelling beasts over the next ridge could the blue coats even approach the battlefield.

Nonetheless, the twelve-man detail from Fort Union would soon render a valuable service. The officer in charge, Captain John Guidry, turned out to be Elena Vargas's fiancé.

Wild Bill sized up the young officer. Guidry was a West Point man, a timberman's son from the placid shores of Lake Erie. Though young and inexperienced, he was also bright and capable. He struck Bill as a fast learner—a good quality for surviving out here. Hickok took him aside.

"Captain, obviously you officially represent the U.S. government. If I turn that bell over to you, I will have fulfilled Sam Baxter's last wish. But the thing of it is, the bell don't really *belong* to our government. Not legally or any way else. Sure, Sam had some tit for tat in mind. But you know what that bell means to the folks in Chimayo—and, of course, to Elena?"

Guidry nodded. "Believe me I know, Wild Bill. It's all she talks about lately."

"So take the bell back to Chimayo and hang it in the belfry at El Santuario. That way, I help Sam, you help Elena and Chimayo. And no regulations broken."

"Yes, sir!"

Guidry's strong white teeth flashed in a wide grin. Everyone knew Wild Bill Hickok was a great favorite with Army brass, including some top generals. Guidry knew he was safe from any disciplinary actions.

However, the young officer indicated the dead bodies with a wave of his arm. "After us soldiers bury this sorry bunch, that is. I'd leave them to the carrion birds, myself. But the Army has to abide by the sanitation code. Burn or bury all human remains."

Bill nodded. "That's always been a problem in my profession," he said with a straight face. "Disposal, I mean. I'm damned if I'll ever bury any man that tried to kill me. I'm a freethinker, but I've got my pride."

* * *

From Chama Bluffs it was only a half day's ride back to the Lazy M. Somehow, though, Wild Bill didn't expect to make it back without one final encounter with Frank Tutt.

Bill was right. About three miles northeast of Pecos, the two horsebackers topped a creosote hill and saw a solitary figure, standing hip-cocked out in the trail ahead of them—obviously waiting. Perhaps five hundred yards still separated them.

"Tutt," Bill said calmly, knocking the long duster away from his Colts. "No tricks this time, junior."

Wild Bill and Josh trotted their mounts perhaps half the distance.

"Far enough, Longfellow," Bill said, reining in. "You wait here. Step well to the side, though."

Bill swung down and handed his reins up to Josh.

"Careful, Bill," the reporter warned. "That holster of his is jury-rigged somehow. I saw some queer-looking rivet deal when I held it at Polvo."

Hickok nodded, adjusting his hat in the glaring, late-afternoon sun. His eyes closed to slits as he watched Tutt approach.

"Yeah? Thanks, kid. I'd figure him for a quick-shot rig. He's a blowhard coward like his brother was. Won't matter, though. Also like his brother, he's about to eat lead."

Josh had seen this cool, unshakable confidence come over Wild Bill before. He feared no man who faced him openly; Hickok had already predicted he would die from a bullet to the back before he turned forty.

The two men advanced closer, heads lowered, hands out at their sides.

"I been waitin' a long time, Hickok!" Tutt shouted.

"Shoulda waited even longer," Bill replied in a quiet voice that nonetheless carried.

Now Josh could make out Tutt's stone-hard eyes and the crooked slash of his mouth.

"You back-shot my brother, you Yankee nigger lover!"

"Not only back-shot him," Bill lied, goading, "but I topped his woman and made him watch me have fun while he died."

Tutt's handsome face crumpled into a mask of rage. "Shut *up*, you disgusting son of a bitch!"

Wild Bill visualized the pain starched into Sam Baxter's dead face. "Know how I'm going to kill you, Frank?" Bill continued to taunt him. "Two slugs about two inches under your belly button. Low in the entrails. It'll hurt like the dickens, but take you hours to bleed out."

Josh saw the color drain from Tutt's face. He stopped, and so did Wild Bill. The two men were now about thirty yards apart. The sound of cicadas seemed to rise to an unbearable shriek in that dust and heat.

"Ah, you're just whistlin' past the graveyard, Hickok! Damn you and all your kin to hell! Make your play!"

"Oh, I'll kill you. But right now I'm enjoying watching you piss yourself like a scared little puppy. The big, bad Tutt boys, white livers all."

That tore it for Frank Tutt. With a snarl of out-of-control rage, he abruptly slapped the butt of his Navy Colt, swiveling the still-holstered weapon up into firing position. And it did go off—but Tutt's slick gadgets could not match Hickok's killer instinct and animal reflexes. As Bill promised, Tutt did indeed have two bullets deep in his guts by the time his gun fired, bucking slightly.

His bullet hornet-buzzed harmlessly past Wild Bill's ear.

Frank crumpled, then writhed in the dirt, moaning piteously and begging for help. Looking disgusted at himself for caving in to pity, Bill walked closer and tossed a finishing shot into Tutt's head.

"I'm getting old, kid," he lamented wearily as he thumbed three reloads into his smoking gun. Then he took his reins back from Josh and swung up and over.

A few days of badly needed recuperation, at Mitt McGinnis's comfortable ranch, put Wild Bill in a more sanguine mood.

So, too, did the surprise messenger sent from Santa Fe by Elena Vargas. The citizens of Chimayo were still celebrating the return of their bell, convinced Wild Bill had broken the dreaded Curse of Hidalgo. Elena and Captain Guidry had rented the La Fonda's fabulous ballroom for a celebration gala next week in Wild Bill and Josh's honor.

"And me and you also get to split these little beauties right down the middle, kid," Wild Bill gloated as he emptied the chamois money pouch Elena had sent. Ten double-eagle gold pieces tumbled out onto the chenille spread of Josh's bed.

"A hundred dollars apiece," Hickok added. "Better than a poke in the eye with a sharp stick, uh?"

"I guess," Josh responded listlessly, hardly even looking at the glittering coins. "I don't deserve half. I ain't *half* the hero you are."

"No, but few men are, kid," Bill pointed out, for he had never been falsely modest about himself. "Listen. When you shot that team horse, you saved the bell. And your shooting saved me on that slope, allowed me to get into firing position below. Top of all that, you took a knife in your hand that might've ended up in my guts instead. You earned your pay."

"Yeah, I s'pose," Josh agreed automatically, picking at a loose thread in the bedspread.

Bill knew damn well what was rankling at the kid. He had struck a spark for Liddy McGinnis. Liddy, however, had set her romantic sights on Wild Bill. Normally, that would just have to be the kid's tough luck—Bill did not practice charity where pretty girls were concerned.

But he thought again about how the plucky kid from Philly had bravely refused to leave Chama Bluffs while he could. *A man doesn't desert his partner; it's just not done.*

Damn it, Hickok, Bill told himself, *you're going to do something "noble," ain't you? You stupid fool.*

That afternoon, while Mitt supervised the dehorning of the yearlings, Bill and Liddy contrived to steal away into the empty library. Liddy looked pretty in a black skirt and a frilly white shirtwaist. Her blond hair fell unrestrained in back, in the bold new fashion Europeans called "the American style."

"Bill?" Liddy said coquettishly. "You said you don't mind it when women presume. Well . . . you know, Elena Vargas has invited Mitt and me to the ball at La Fonda."

"Of course," Bill said, subtly drawing Liddy with him into the bay of a window that overlooked the front yard. "I hope my name will be first on your dance card?"

"I was hoping," Liddy told him, lowering her eyes modestly, "it would also be *last*."

Both of them knew the custom. The last name listed on a lady's dance card was also her official escort for the evening—a fact routinely reported in the "society pages." And the name of any woman escorted by Wild Bill would go out over the wires, including the new Transatlantic Cable.

Bill ignored her hint. Outside, a despondent-looking Josh was sitting on the top rail of the breaking pen, watching the peelers break wild broncos to leather.

"Joshua pretty much figures the stars rise from your eyes," Bill remarked casually. "And he told me you have a voice like waltzing violins."

"Josh said that? Why, how poetic!" Liddy's eyes cut thoughtfully to the window. "He's a sweet boy."

"Boy? Oh, hey! Take a better look at him, Liddy. Sure, his grammar is perfect; he's a bang-up newspaperman. But he's also all grit in a scrape. He faced death on Chama Bluffs and didn't blink once. Know why? He wanted you to be proud of him."

"He did?"

"I should say! He even told me he wasn't afraid to die—not when Liddy McGinnis proved there were angels."

"Why . . . that sweet poet," Liddy said, watching Joshua in earnest now.

"Yeah," Wild Bill went on, slyly playing to the "nest-building" instinct in most females. "A girl can have a good time with me, all right. But she can build a *family* with a man like that."

"Yes," Liddy said softly, still watching Joshua. He *was* a handsome lad, especially in sad profile like this. He looked. . . . emotionally turbulent. That appealed to a high-strung girl like Liddy.

"Maybe," she suggested, as if it were her idea, "I can ask Joshua to be my escort?"

"Excellent idea," Bill approved. He was already edging toward the door, tempted by the intoxicating lilac smell of Liddy's perfume—and the generous swell of her heaving bosom. It wouldn't do to seduce Josh's new lady love.

Just as Bill excused himself and started to open the door, Liddy's voice stopped him.

"Bill? It's not . . . me, is it?" She cast her eyes down and flushed. "Do you find me desirable enough?"

Bill took in those polished-apple cheeks and cornflower blue eyes, the heart-shaped lips made for endless kisses. He shut the door with his heel.

"Come on over here," he dared her, his voice suddenly husky, "and I'll show you how desirable you are. I've already seen you naked, in my thoughts, and I like what I saw."

His bluntness shocked her so much that Liddy was forced to grab the back of the nearest chair. "Bill! My lands, you're shameless! You've . . . why, I can hardly catch a breath!"

Bill laughed. "You hot little firecracker! You'll eat the kid alive and spit out his bones. But what a way to go."

His mission complete, Hickok was about to open the door. But Liddy called his name again.

"Bill? Yesterday I talked to Martha Jane. Is it true she saved your life at Chama Bluffs?"

Liddy had a sly look on her face. Bill didn't like the turn this trail was taking.

"She's saved it more than once," he conceded reluctantly.

"Yes. Because she's so sweet on you."

Bill started to shake his head, for he had caught

Liddy's drift. Sure, Calamity Jane saved his bacon. But her face terrified buzzards. And the smell coming off her could raise blood blisters on new leather.

"Oh no you don't, Liddy. I'm grateful, but not crazy."

"The newspapers call you a gentleman, Bill Hickok. Gentlemen do the noble thing."

"Absolutely not," Bill insisted. "It won't happen. Me, take Jane to a dance? It's like pouring kerosene on a wildfire."

Liddy flashed a coy smile. "Sorry, Bill. It's a deal-breaker, as my brother says. If I go with Joshua, you go with Martha."

"It won't happen," Bill repeated stubbornly. "The woman is a cannibal! Absolutely not, I'm telling you.

By the time the night for feting Wild Bill had arrived, speculation was intense: *Which* beautiful, exotic woman would end up on the arm of the dashing Hickok?

The carriage from the Lazy M arrived fashionably late. The ballroom was full, and the guest-of-honor table already crowded. Its occupants included Elena in an elegant silk sheath; Captain Guidry in his dress blues; and the mayor of Santa Fe, wearing long tails and a topper.

A delighted murmur rolled through the grand ballroom when Joshua, with Liddy on his arm, entered from the lobby. Liddy's emerald-green gown sparkled under the chandeliers. Next came Mitt, with a popular local schoolteacher on his arm.

And a moment later, the guest of honor himself. Wild Bill wore his new black wool suit. But he hadn't bothered with his guns tonight because the proudly beaming woman on his arm wore hers.

"It's Calamity Jane!" exclaimed a dumbfounded East Coast newspaperman. "In a *dress!* Well, that gets *my* money!"

Jane's calico dress looked more like a sack than a dress, and barely covered her stout limbs. She still wore her beloved John B. Stetson. And to protect Bill, her Smith & Wesson protruded from the sash around her waist.

"Wine?" Jane snorted with contempt when a white-jacketed steward hovered at her elbow, ready to pour. "Hell, honey, wine is just vinegar sneaking up on old age! Bring me some whiskey. Rotgut will do just fine."

Several reporters stood along the walls, furiously taking notes. One was red-faced from drinking all evening.

"Hey, Jane!" he roared out in the quiet ballroom. "Is it true those camels of yours love you so much because they see their mothers in your face?"

Jane was on her best behavior. But suddenly she had sand in her ointment. The pistol filled her hand before Bill could move to stop her.

"By grab, mister," she retorted, thumbing the weapon to full cock, "they're going to see *daylight* in yours, you milk-kneed gal-boy!"

Bill grabbed the muzzle. "Apologize real nice, mister, and I won't let her kill you."

The reporter stammered his regrets, mollifying Jane. But before a half hour had passed, she had emptied her first bottle of whiskey.

"Hey!" she hollered down the table so Josh and Liddy, busy whispering to each other, could hear her. So could everyone else. "You two aim to pitch a little hay tonight?"

Liddy didn't understand the phrase, but Josh flushed deep. Before he could recover, Jane added, addressing the entire ballroom: "Bill told me Joshua here ain't never had his clock wound. Hell, he's still on ma's milk!"

The La Fonda erupted in laughter. Bill, too, laughed until tears streamed from his eyes.

This is more like it, he told himself as he returned the wink of a sassy redhead across the room. Finally I'm having some *fun*.

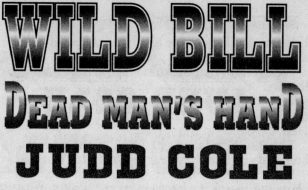

WILD BILL

JUDD COLE

THE KINKAID COUNTY WAR

Wild Bill Hickok is a legend in his own lifetime. Wherever he goes his reputation with a gun precedes him—along with an open bounty of $10,000 for his arrest. But Wild Bill is working for the law when he goes to Kinkaid County, Wyoming. Hundreds of prime longhorn cattle have been poisoned, and Bill is sent by the Pinkerton Agency to get to the bottom of it. He doesn't expect to land smack dab in the middle of an all-out range war, but that's exactly what happens. With the powerful Cattleman's Association on one side and land-grant settlers on the other, Wild Bill knows that before this is over he'll be testing his gun skills to the limit if he hopes to get out alive.

___4529-X $3.99 US/$4.99 CAN

CHEYENNE

BLOODY BONES CANYON/ RENEGADE SIEGE

JUDD COLE

Bloody Bones Canyon. Only Touch the Sky can defend them from the warriors that threaten to take over the camp. But when his people need him most, the mighty shaman is forced to avenge the slaughter of their peace chief. Even Touch the Sky cannot fight two battles at once, and without his powerful magic his people will be doomed.

And in the same action-packed volume . . .

Renegade Siege. Touch the Sky's blood enemies have surrounded a pioneer mining camp and are preparing to sweep down on it like a killing wind. If the mighty shaman cannot hold off the murderous attack, the settlers will be wiped out . . . and Touch the Sky's own camp will be next!

___4586-9 $4.99 US/$5.99 CAN

CHEYENNE

VENGEANCE QUEST/ WARRIOR FURY

JUDD COLE

Vengeance Quest. When his cunning rivals kill a loyal friend in their quest to create a renegade nation, Touch the Sky sets out on a bloody trail that will lead to either revenge on his hated foes—or his own savage death.

And in the same action-packed volume . . .

Warrior Fury. After luring Touch the Sky away from the Cheyenne camp, murderous backshooters dare to kidnap his wife and newborn son. If Touch the Sky fails to save his family, he will kill his foes with his bare hands—then spend eternity walking an endless trail of tears.

___4531-1 $4.99 US/$5.99 CAN

CHEYENNE

JUDD COLE

Follow the adventures of Touch the Sky as he searches for a world he can call his own!

#3: Renegade Justice. When his adopted white parents fall victim to a gang of ruthless outlaws, Touch the Sky swears to save them—even if it means losing the trust he has risked his life to win from the Cheyenne.

_3385-2 $3.50 US/$4.50 CAN

#4: Vision Quest. While seeking a mystical sign from the Great Spirit, Touch the Sky is relentlessly pursued by his enemies. But the young brave will battle any peril that stands between him and the vision of his destiny.

_3411-5 $3.50 US/$4.50 CAN

CHEYENNE

DOUBLE EDITION
JUDD COLE

One man's heroic search for a world he can call his own.

Arrow Keeper. A Cheyenne raised among pioneers, Matthew Hanchon has never known anything but distrust. The settlers brand him a savage, and when Matthew realizes that his adopted parents will suffer for his sake, he flees into the wilderness—where he'll need a warrior's courage if he hopes to survive.

And in the same volume...

Death Chant. When Matthew returns to the Cheyenne, he doesn't find the acceptance he seeks. The Cheyenne can't fully trust any who were raised in the ways of the white man. Forced to prove his loyalty, Matthew faces the greatest challenge he has ever known.

___4280-0 $4.99 US/$5.99 CAN

CHEYENNE

Spirit Path
Mankiller
Judd Cole

Spirit Path. The mighty Cheyenne trust their tribe's shaman to protect them against great sickness and bloody defeat. A rival accuses Touch the Sky of bad medicine, and if he can't prove the claim false, he'll come to a brutal end.

And in the same action-packed volume . . .

Mankiller. A fierce warrior, Touch the Sky can outfight, outwit, and outlast any enemy. Yet the fearsome Cherokee brave named Mankiller can snap a man's neck as easily as a reed, and he is determined to count coup on Touch the Sky.

___4445-5 $4.99 US/$5.99 CAN

Dorchester Publishing Co., Inc.
P.O. Box 6640
Wayne, PA 19087-8640

Please add $1.75 for shipping and handling for the first book and $.50 for each book thereafter. NY, NYC, and PA residents, please add appropriate sales tax. No cash, stamps, or C.O.D.s. All orders shipped within 6 weeks via postal service book rate. Canadian orders require $2.00 extra postage and must be paid in U.S. dollars through a U.S. banking facility.

Name_____
Address_____
City_____ State_____ Zip_____
I have enclosed $_____ in payment for the checked book(s).
Payment <u>must</u> accompany all orders. ❑ Please send a free catalog.
      CHECK OUT OUR WEBSITE! www.dorchesterpub.com

CHEYENNE
WENDIGO MOUNTAIN
DEATH CAMP
JUDD COLE

Wendigo Mountain. A Cheyenne warrior raised by white settlers, Touch the Sky is blessed with strong medicine. Yet his powers as a shaman cannot help him foretell that his tribe's sacred arrows will be stolen—or that his enemies will demand his head for their return. To save his tribe from utter destruction, the young brave will wage a battle like none he's ever fought.

And in the same action-packed volume . . .

Death Camp. Touch the Sky will gladly give his life to protect his tribe. Yet not even he can save them from an outbreak of deadly disease. Racing against time and brutal enemies, Touch the Sky has to either forsake his heritage and trust the white man's medicine—or prove his loyalty even as he watches his proud people die.

___4479-X $4.99 US/$5.99 CAN

Dorchester Publishing Co., Inc.
P.O. Box 6640
Wayne, PA 19087-8640

Please add $1.75 for shipping and handling for the first book and $.50 for each book thereafter. NY, NYC, and PA residents, please add appropriate sales tax. No cash, stamps, or C.O.D.s. All orders shipped within 6 weeks via postal service book rate. Canadian orders require $2.00 extra postage and must be paid in U.S. dollars through a U.S. banking facility.

Name_____
Address_____
City_____State_____Zip_____
I have enclosed $_____ in payment for the checked book(s).
Payment <u>must</u> accompany all orders. ❏ Please send a free catalog.
    CHECK OUT OUR WEBSITE! www.dorchesterpub.com

CHEYENNE

RENEGADE NATION
ORPHAN TRAIN
JUDD COLE

Renegade Nation. Born the son of a great chief, raised by frontier settlers, Touch the Sky will never forsake his pioneer friends in their time of need. Then Touch the Sky's enemies join forces against all his people—both Indian and white. If the fearless brave's magic is not strong enough, he will be powerless to stop the annihilation of the two worlds he loves. *And in the same action-packed volume . . .*

Orphan Train. When his enemies kidnap a train full of orphans heading west, the young shaman finds himself torn between the white men and the Indians. To save the children, the mighty warrior will have to risk his life, his home, and his dreams of leading his tribe to glory.